AFTER THE HARVEST

Clare Mountjoy must leave the mill-house when her grandmother dies. But, given work as a governess, she moves into Abinger Hall — home of the new Squire, Howard Tregarth, who has inherited his uncle's estate in the West Country. When she occupies the reputedly haunted Blue Room she wonders where the sobbing comes from late at night. Why does she have an enemy in the house? And what is the truth behind the terrifying secret of the Blue Room?

LILLIE HOLLAND

AFTER THE HARVEST

Complete and Unabridged

LINFORD
Leicester

First published in Great Britain in 1978

First Linford Edition
published 2011

British Library CIP Data

Holland, Lillie.
After the harvest. - -
(Linford romance library)
1. Governesses- -Fiction. 2. Gentry- -
Fiction. 3. Haunted houses- -Fiction.
4. Love stories. 5. Large type books.
I. Title II. Series
823.9′2–dc22

ISBN 978–1–4448–0796–7

Published by
F. A. Thorpe (Publishing)
Anstey, Leicestershire

Set by Words & Graphics Ltd.
Anstey, Leicestershire
Printed and bound in Great Britain by
T. J. International Ltd., Padstow, Cornwall

This book is printed on acid-free paper

1

I sat in the kitchen of the mill-house, with the letter from Howard Tregarth on the scrubbed deal table in front of me. It seemed to be the last straw in what had been a disastrous year up to now.

I had never set eyes on 'the young Squire', as the villagers called him. Not that I had ever set eyes on his uncle, 'the old Squire'. He had never shown himself in the village of Bramwell for years before his death. Abinger Hall, the Tregarths' home, was a couple of miles out of the village, private, remote, and inaccessible. It was rumoured to be an unlucky place, and they were considered an unlucky family.

They were unlucky! With bitterness in my heart, I re-read that letter.

'Dear Miss Mountjoy', it ran, 'I understand that your family has rented the mill-house for a long time, but that the mill itself has been unused for about twenty years. It is not my wish that this state of affairs should continue. By rights, the mill-house and mill are rented together. I intend to put a miller in the house in due course. I understand that your grandmother has recently died, leaving you there alone. I would not have pressed this matter during her lifetime, and I am sorry to hear of your loss, but I am afraid I must now give you notice to quit the premises. Naturally, I do not wish to cause you any hardship. As is the custom, you will not be asked to vacate the premises until after the harvest. But please take notice that I want the mill-house vacant as soon as possible, after harvesting has been completed.'

It was signed Howard Tregarth.

I had heard that he was going to make sweeping changes on the estate, so long neglected by old Lionel Tregarth. It seemed that I was going to be part of them — as if my problems were not pressing enough at the moment. I rose and walked over to the window. A shaft of pale spring sunshine broke through the clouds, and shone on the wet green grass and clumps of daffodils in the long, sloping mill-house garden. I fought back the tears as I thought how my grandmother had loved that garden. It was only two months since she had died, and the sense of her presence still lingered around the place.

True, I had been away for nearly two years, employed as a governess with a family in Plymouth. It had been a good, well paid post, although at first I had been reluctant to take it. It had been my mother's wish that I should do so, before her death nearly three years ago. She had been the village schoolmistress, and she had taught me well. After I was sixteen, I assisted her in the school, but it had not been her wish that I should remain there. She wanted me to take a post away from the village, even though she must have known it meant leaving my grandmother alone. It had been a big wrench for me to do that, but Gran had been very unselfish about it.

'You must go, my love. I have a few friends, and Old Mollie will be here to tend me if need be. And there is always home for you to come back to. Your mother wanted you to have an opportunity to see a little of life away from the village.'

Well, I had done that, and even managed to send my grandmother money home. I knew that she must have missed me terribly when I first went away. Yet she had carried on uncomplainingly until the beginning of the year, when I had come home, and found her failing fast. I knew then that I would have to leave the Thomas family, and stay with her to the end. My employers, although reluctant to lose me, were very understanding. They generously sent me a month's salary.

They had a new schoolmistress at the village school, but the parson's two young daughters had received tuition from me every day. I had divided my time between teaching them and nursing my grandmother. Old Mollie had assisted me with the tasks at home as much as possible, but she was not as nimble as formerly. She had been called Old Mollie ever since I could remember, but now the name fitted her. She was a strange, solitary sort of woman, white-haired, hook-nosed, witchlike in appearance. I knew that the village children were afraid of her, but she had always been good to my grandmother, and kind to me, too.

For many years she had been the local midwife, always in demand for births and deaths, and sick people. Her cottage was a few yards further along the river bank; like our house, set well away from the village itself.

I stood at the window, considering the hopelessness of my position. I no longer had the parson's children to teach, as they had moved to another living in the north just a month before. I was without a post, almost without money, and without any family to care about what happened to me. After the harvest I would be without a home, too . . .

I picked up the letter, and put on my black cloak. I had few clothes, and what I had were plain and serviceable. My grandmother had told me not to wear mourning for her longer than two months. And later, towards the end, she had murmured: 'You've been a good girl — a good girl . . . ' Her last words were so strange that I thought of them again, as I prepared to go out.

'Unconsecrated ground,' she had whispered. 'Like a dog . . . '

I blinked away my sudden tears, and locked the door of the mill-house behind me. A corn dolly hung over the porch for luck. Luck, I thought to myself bitterly. Was there such a thing? As soon as he heard the mill-house door being closed, Barnaby, my old bloodhound, came from the back of the house, where he had been lurking.

He gave a couple of barks, and

walked with me along the rather muddy river path towards Mollie's cottage. Barnaby had been a puppy when I had been a child, and he was a great comfort to me. He guarded both the mill-house and Mollie's cottage, for which she was grateful, and gave him many bones and titbits. She greeted me at the door of her house.

'I thought 'ee would be coming, my lovely,' she said. I entered the cottage with Barnaby at my heels. The cottage had only one door, and that faced on to the river. Mollie's garden was a wild tangle of weeds, grass, and choked flowers battling to survive. The one outstanding feature which it boasted was a fine weeping willow tree which hung right over into the water.

'I've had a letter from the young Squire, Mr. Tregarth,' I said, holding it up. 'He's given me notice to leave the house after the harvest. He wants to put a miller in the mill-house, and see the mill put to proper use again. I don't know what to do. I suppose I must find a situation somewhere. But it means I shall have no home at all to come back to — ' I broke off, unable to continue. Mollie made sympathetic noises, and after a few moments, I read the letter to her. She sat thinking it over.

'You could come here,' she said finally. 'This be a bigger house than it looks outside. The attics would take some furniture, and there be a spare bedroom for you.'

I'd had a feeling that she might make this suggestion. It was kind of her, and it was true that her thatched cottage was roomy enough to accommodate me, and some of the furniture from the mill-house. I really didn't want to make my home with Mollie, though, not even as a temporary measure.

'The old Squire would have let me stay,' I said bitterly. 'He never bothered people.'

'He never bothered about nothing, my love.' Mollie began to tell me about her leaking roof, and of the many repairs she had never had done, and how it was the same everywhere in the village. 'But the young Squire, they do say he gets things done,' she finished vaguely. 'Anyway, 'ee couldn't go on living there alone.'

'Why not? You live alone — my grandmother lived alone.'

'Yes, but I'm old.'

'You've lived alone for years, though, ever since you were widowed,' I pursued.

'Ah, I bain't never been pretty, though. 'Tis not safe when it's known around the district that a girl like you is alone in the mill-house. With your white skin and blue eyes, and hair that moves like ivy leaves when you let it down — you mark my words, there's more than one young man will be hanging around the mill-house.'

'They'll get a warm reception from Barnaby if they do,' I said. 'Anyway, young men are not my problem at the moment. Wherever I live, I shall have to find a situation as soon as possible.'

Mollie nodded sympathetically, and

we sat and talked about it for some time.

'I've a mind to go and see the Squire myself,' I said. 'Why should I have to put up with being treated thus?'

' 'Tis hard, my pretty. But he be the Squire.' Mollie had the patient, countrywoman's acceptance of such things. But I had lived for two years in the bustling, busy, city of Plymouth, and I knew that people had different ideas in towns.

'I shall go and see him,' I repeated uncertainly.

'You would never dare.'

'Why not? What have I to lose? He's given me notice to quit.'

'You be a sharp maid. Well, go and tell 'un, then.' She gave me an admiring glance. 'Jennie would have been proud to hear you talk so.' She meant my grandmother.

'I miss her,' I said.

'Yes, and it's brave of you to stay in that house alone now.'

'I can't understand what Gran meant

before she died, Mollie. You had gone for the doctor. I bent down to catch what she was saying, and it sounded like 'unconsecrated ground' and 'like a dog'. I couldn't bring myself to mention it before. What did she mean, I wonder?'

'Wandering in her mind, I expect,' said the old woman. 'I haven't been to the well today, yet. I must go.'

'Yes, I need fresh water, too,' I said, preparing to leave. Barnaby stood up, ready to go with me.

Back in the mill-house, I looked at a big key hanging from a hook in the kitchen. It had hung there ever since I could remember. On a sudden impulse I took it down. I knew that the mill had been shut up for years, since before I was born, in fact. Mountjoys had always been at the mill, but my father had died suddenly, three months before my birth. Since then it had just been left. I knew that my mother had been a governess, a north country girl who had met the young miller while employed with one of the local families. She had married him against the wishes of her own family, and had broken all ties with them.

My father had lived with his widowed mother in the mill-house, and after her son's marriage she had still continued to live there with the young couple. It had proved a good arrangement after my birth. My mother earned a living as the village schoolmistress, and my grandmother cared for me in her absence. My grandmother also kept hens, tended her vegetable garden, and ensured that we lived as well and cheaply as possible. There were no other Mountjoys in the village, and although my mother was well known in the district, she was never one of the villagers. She kept herself a little apart, always, and from an early age I had not been encouraged to mix too freely with them. As the mill-house was some way from the village, this had not been too difficult.

Going away as a governess after her

death had increased my sense of isolation from the villagers. They considered me 'different', I knew. After all, my mother was an educated woman who could speak French, and play the piano, and she had taught me these accomplishments. So even if she had married the miller, she was not one of the villagers, nor was I. There were no strong ties, really, to bind me to Bramwell now my grandmother was gone. I thought of the villagers; red-cheeked, cider-drinking, good-natured yokels for the most part. I had nothing against them, but the idea of marrying one of them was utterly distasteful. I wondered if something of that sort had crossed my mother's mind during her last illness. Was that why she had wanted me to leave the village? It seemed to me I was in a hopeless position. I had very little money, I was soon to have no home, and I had no relatives. I was far from being a simple village maid, and yet, I was but the daughter of a miller. I seemed to fit nowhere in the scheme of things.

With the mill key in my hand, I left the house, and walked to the deserted mill, with Barnaby loping along beside me. As a child I had always been a bit afraid of the place. Weeds and green slime clung to the motionless mill-wheel; as I approached the door I felt a twinge of the old fear, mingled with curiosity. I put the key in the lock, and turned it slowly, but it was far too stiff.

'Can I help?' came a man's voice, and Barnaby gave a few barks. With a start I turned and saw George Hansbury, the saddler, watching me. He was a burly man of about fifty, fair-haired and red-faced, wearing a leathern jacket and corduroy trousers. 'I was passing by,' he continued, and after a slight hesitation added 'miss'.

'Oh, no thank you,' I said, in some confusion. He was a nice man, kind and gentle, and very respected in the village.

'Do you want it opened?' he continued, walking up to me, while Barnaby

14

growled suspiciously.

'It's not important,' I said. 'The place hasn't been opened for years.'

'They say not. But I'll open him for 'ee.' He took the key in his hand, and screwing up his face, exerted considerable strength, so much so that I thought the key would break in the lock. Instead, it turned; he put his hand on the great door and pushed. It yielded, and opening creakingly, it displayed the dark and abandoned interior of the mill. There was an overpowering smell of rottenness; instinctively I recoiled from it.

'It do smell,' said George Hansbury, with a laugh. 'Nothing here to frighten 'un, though.' He appeared to be extremely interested. Rotting sacks lay on the floor, ragged and covered in cobwebs.

'They say everything was left, just as it was,' I murmured, half to myself.

'The rats will have eaten any meal around — every grain, yes, I know them. Gnawed the sacks, too,' commented my companion. The windows were dim with dirt; shafts of spring sunlight filtered through, making great beams of dust. Wooden steps led up to the millstones.

'There's another floor,' I said.

'Yes, but don't go up they steps, miss ... It'll need a deal of work doing — '

'What do you mean?' I asked.

'Well, they do say — I had heard as the young Squire wants to get the mill working again, and put a miller in the mill-house.'

So already there were whispers in the village.

'Be it true?' he asked gently, compassion in his honest blue eyes.

'Yes, it's true,' I said.

'What will you do, then?' he asked. It was really none of his concern, but he was so kind that I could scarcely tell him so. We stepped outside the mill, and he carefully locked the door behind us.

'I don't really know what I shall do,' I said lightly. 'I have plenty of time to make up my mind — several months, in fact. Probably I shall take a post away again.' In silence I walked along the muddy path to the mill-house, with him beside me. I turned in at the gate.

'If you need a bit of company, miss,' he said awkwardly, 'my wife would be glad to see you. And my daughter, Polly.'

'Thank you,' I said. 'You are very kind. I must go inside now. Good day.'

He stood watching me as I let myself into the mill-house. I had known his daughter, Polly, from when she was at school. She was a pretty girl, a bit younger than myself. Once or twice as a child, I had played with Polly, and I remembered their cramped little parlour behind the shop.

Inside the stone-flagged mill-house kitchen, I looked around with a critical eye. Gran had neglected everything during the past year, although I had put up new gingham curtains, and done my best to make the place look more attractive. There were holes in the plaster, and the window sashes needed renewing. One of the window panes had been cracked for months.

I went into the parlour. On the wall there was a faded sepia photograph of my father as a young man, in what was obviously his best suit. There was a stuffed fox under a glass dome, two very old leather armchairs, and a completely threadbare carpet. The room boasted a piano, which needed tuning rather badly. A little table and a workbox comprised most of the remaining furniture. There were two equally shabby bedrooms on the next floor, two almost empty ones above that, and then a large attic. I picked up a pitcher, and left the house again, this time for water. The well, a few yards from the house, was only used by me and Mollie.

For the rest of the day, I busied myself about the house. Later, I washed my long, black hair, and lit the fire in the parlour, so that I could dry it. Although my hair was so dark, my eyes were blue, not brown, as might be expected, especially as my mother's eyes had been dark. She told me that she had never been really pretty, but that my father had been a handsome man, and indeed, he appeared so on the photograph.

Later, in the glow of the oil lamp, I tried to read a book which I had bought in Plymouth, and forgotten about until I had found it unexpectedly while busy in the house that day. After a while, I put it down, and sat with my thoughts. If I could find a post where I could teach somewhere during the day, and come home at night, that would be ideal. But I couldn't come home at night, because soon I wouldn't have a home — wouldn't have anywhere I could call my own. And what would become of Barnaby?

The young Squire, indeed! Then I remembered how I had told Old Mollie that I would go and see him about that letter I had received. I hadn't really meant it at the time, as the prospect was somewhat daunting. Now, however, resentment against him reached boiling point within me. Why shouldn't I go and see him? Even if he were angry, it would make no difference. I would go and tell him what I thought of him. I knew where Abinger Hall was. It had a pretty sandstone lodge at the entrance gates, and there was a long drive up to the house. The drive curved, so I had never actually seen the house itself.

Suppose I went, and the Squire was not in, or would not see me? Suppose . . . suppose . . .

I sat there, musing about first one thing, and then another. At last I took a lamp, and led the way to my bedroom, with Barnaby pattering after me. I made my toilet, and climbed into bed. Barnaby scrambled up after me. I should not have allowed him on the bed; Gran never would. But what did it matter now? I was safe with him beside me, and the sound of his breathing close to me gave me the only real comfort I had experienced that day.

2

The following morning I set off for Abinger Hall. I wore my black cloak and bonnet, and a grey dress. It had been raining, but it was dry and sunny now. I listened to the birdsong as I walked along, and looked at the spring flowers growing in the hedgerows. One or two of the villagers saw me, and bade me good day.

As I went along I rehearsed what I was going to say, although I was not really sure what to say. I wanted to stay in the mill-house, but even if I did, I would have to earn money in order to live. I was prepared to go away if necessary, but I wanted the mill-house to come back to sometimes. I just wanted it to be waiting for me. I knew that Old Mollie would keep an eye on things, and have Barnaby as well.

It was sheep washing time, and I

could hear the animals bleating from the water meadow beside the river, where there was a pool used for this purpose. At the end of the twisting, hilly lane out of the village, I took the turn to the right, with fields on either side, and thickly wooded slopes in the distance. My mind was in a state of turmoil as I walked along. I had enjoyed living in Plymouth, and yet I had always been pleased to come home. The Thomas family had another governess, I knew, otherwise I could have gone back to them. It was not the leaving of Bramwell that troubled me as much as having no home to come back to.

It was spring now; soon it would be summer, and then harvest time. And after the harvest, what then? I heard the sound of hooves behind me, and turning round I saw a waggon approaching rapidly. I guessed it would be going with goods of some sort to Chollerford market. The waggoner had his wife beside him. He reined in the horse as they drew level, and they both smiled at me.

'Good day, my love. I be going to Chollerford market; if you be going, I'll take you there,' he said.

It was a tempting offer. He was a middle-aged man, fresh-faced and jolly looking, and his wife was a plump, apple-cheeked woman, dressed obviously in her Sunday clothes, for some reason.

'Thank you. If you could take me as far as the crossroads, I should be grateful,' I said. I climbed up beside them.

'I be going to stay with my sister,' said his wife, as he clucked the horse on again. 'Be you going far?'

'I'm going in the direction of Abinger Hall,' I replied.

'Ah! That lies the other way. They say we mun all expect changes now young Squire has come to live in these parts. I say he don't own us, but Dick do say he owns a lot of the land, and it might not be bad if he sees to some of the things the old Squire did nothing about. My mother worked up at the Hall when she was young, and told me about the goings-on there. Young Squire be widowed, bain't he?'

'I don't know,' I said. 'I know nothing about him. I've been away from these parts for some time.'

'Been away, eh? We don't live right in Bramwell, but they say the young Squire lived abroad, and his wife died, and left 'un with a little maid to bring up. Old Squire had a broken heart for years on account of his son.'

'I've heard they are an unlucky family,' I said.

'They do say the place be haunted — that the ghost of a young woman sobs in one of the rooms. I don't know if it be true or not, but I have heard that the old Squire's son married a foreigner against his father's wishes, and died in some foreign place. Old Squire shut himself away for years.'

'That's true,' I said. 'I've never seen him.'

'You live in Bramwell, then?'

'Yes,' I answered, a little hesitantly, as the waggoner's wife seemed such a gossip.

'It's a good spring,' was her next remark. 'Plenty of rain, but sunshine too. It makes for a good harvest, Dick do say.' She chattered on in like manner until we reached the crossroads. Her husband said little; he was probably accustomed to her constant talking.

'Glad to have helped 'ee, my love,' he said, when I alighted at the crossroads.

'Thank you. Good day,' I said. His wife waved to me, and I smiled at her and waved back. I stood for a moment, watching the waggon drive away. There was a wooden signpost with 'Choller-ford' painted on it, and a religious text painted on the road by what appeared to be the same hand. Three lanes met here. One went to the village, one to Chollerford, and the third branched off, and went past the Squire's house.

Nervously, I began to walk along. Cattle were grazing in the meadows on either side, and ahead I could see a wood, and a high stone wall. I knew that the wall enclosed the Squire's parkland and house. I felt more nervous with every step I took. At last I reached the sandstone lodge cottage, and the great, wrought iron gates. I was immediately seen; a young woman appeared at the door of the cottage, clutching a baby in her arms. She looked at me enquiringly.

'Good day. I have business with Mr. Tregarth,' I said brightly.

To my tremendous surprise and relief, she merely nodded, and opened one side of the gate to allow me through. Before me lay a long, curving drive, with trees on either side. I turned round and looked back, and to my chagrin I saw the lodge-keeper's wife watching me through the gates. But soon the curve in the drive rendered that impossible, and some way ahead of me, I saw Abinger Hall itself. It looked large and dignified, built in the local sandstone, with an imposing terrace in front, and steps going up to the door. As I drew nearer, I noticed that the balustrade was broken in parts, and that although the flower beds and lawns in front of the house bore signs of recent attention, they fell far short of what I had expected.

Feeling very alone and insignificant, I walked up the steps to the front door. I reached up to pull the great bell, then hesitated. Would it be better to bang with the huge iron knocker? In the end I used the bell, but it seemed I had scarcely touched it before the door opened, and a black-clad footman stood there. His sweeping glance seemed to take in everything about me, my nervousness, my shabbiness, and my complete lack of confidence.

'Good day. Er — I wish to see Mr. Tregarth,' I said falteringly.

'Your name, miss?'

'Miss Mountjoy. I wish to speak to him about business matters.'

The footman raised his eyebrows. 'Is Mr. Tregarth expecting you?'

'No,' I admitted. 'But I am sure he will see me. Tell him that it's about the mill-house.'

After some hesitation on his part, I was allowed inside the house. The footman indicated a chair in the great hall, and I sat down, feeling ready to faint from sheer nervousness. How elegant and beautiful it was inside, with the most exquisite wood carving I had ever seen in my life. Four splendid pillars of dark green marble ran from floor to ceiling, and the staircase was impressive.

The fire was unlit in the great fireplace, where the firedogs and brasses gleamed. The grandfather clock chimed the hour, making me start. There was a faint smell of beeswax, which mingled with the perfume from the hot house flowers arranged on the long oak table. There was not a sign of life about. After what seemed hours, the footman returned.

'Will you come this way, miss? Mr. Tregarth will see you in the library.'

Quaking, I followed him out of the hall, and into a passage. He knocked on a door, opened it for me, and then withdrew, closing it behind him. I was in a room which smelled faintly of cigar smoke. I noticed that the walls were lined with books, and there was a cheerful fire. A man was sitting beside it in a leather armchair, and the first thing I was aware of were his keen grey eyes.

'Good day. Be seated,' he said, almost brusquely, indicating a chair the other side of the fireplace. 'You are Miss — '

'Clare Mountjoy, sir,' I said hastily. I had brought his letter with me, and I held it up. 'I received this letter from you, saying that I shall have to leave the mill-house after the harvest.'

'So you are the tenant actually living in the mill-house now?' He seemed slightly taken aback. I had a feeling he had imagined me to be more of a cottage maid than I was. And now that I was finally face to face with him, my nervousness seemed to go, and I found fresh courage.

'I have had a very bad year up to now,' I said, and my voice was quite composed. 'I had a position as governess with a family who live in Plymouth. When my grandmother became ill, I was obliged to give it up, and come home to nurse her. I did so, until she died. That was a few weeks ago, and now I am told I must quit the house — '

'I have no wish to cause you hardship,' said Mr. Tregarth, briskly. 'The facts of the matter are that my uncle did nothing for the villagers for many years. As I am now living in Abinger Hall, I intend to change things. It is right that corn should be milled here. You surely have relatives in the village with whom you could stay?'

'No. I have none.'

'Friends, then?'

'We have never really had close friends in the village,' I said. 'The mill-house is a bit set apart. There is only Mrs. Treen, who used to help my grandmother, and who lives near me in a cottage. But in any event, sir, I have no wish to live in someone else's house.'

'But you have done that before, as a governess.'

'Yes, but I had a home to come back to. I have been giving lessons to the parson's children, but as you know, we have a new parson now.'

'You mean,' he said thoughtfully, 'that you are now without a post, and shortly to be without a home?'

'It seems so, sir,' I replied. How easy life was for him, I thought. He had so much; position, wealth, and power — the power to make or break the tenants on his land. He appeared to be in his early thirties. He was brown-haired and clean-shaven, and his features were regular. He was, in fact, a handsome man, but I had a feeling he did not smile very easily.

'I did not know all the circumstances before,' he said. 'I think we could come to some arrangement about offering you other accommodation. There must be plenty of empty cottages in the village, places in need of repair, no doubt. If I agreed to have one of them repaired for you, you could make it your home. But I understand that is only part of your problem.'

Strictly speaking, it was the only part which concerned him, but something in his manner intimated that he was prepared to hear more.

'Yes,' I said quietly. 'I am without a post. I shall have to find a position as a governess. I would like one near Bramwell if possible, but even if I have to go some distance away, I won't mind as long as I have a place of my own to come back to.'

The Squire appeared to be thinking deeply. He rose with a sudden, restless movement, and walked over to the window. After staring through it without speaking, he swung round and faced me.

'I have a young daughter,' he said abruptly. 'She is having no tuition at the moment. I intend to engage a governess for her. I am not promising anything, but if your references are satisfactory, I could offer you a post here.'

'Oh!' I was completely taken by surprise. What a strange, unexpected turn my visit to Abinger Hall had taken. A post as governess to the Squire's daughter!

'Have you walked here from the village?' he enquired, suddenly changing the subject.

'Yes, apart from a waggoner giving me a ride to the crossroads.'

He frowned when I said that. 'I wish young women were not so trusting. I am a magistrate, and I see a great deal of the less pleasant side of human nature when I am sitting on the bench. It is foolish to accept rides like that from strange men.'

'His wife was with him, sir,' I said, in a very small voice.

'That is different, then,' he admitted. 'But I shall have you driven back in the dogcart.'

'There is really no need — ' I began,

but he had clearly made up his mind.

'You must be driven back. And the dogcart will call to bring you here tomorrow. Bring any references you may have — I take it you have some?'

'I have one from the family I was with for two years, and one from the parson,' I said.

I could feel my cheeks burning with excitement. At that moment the door burst open, and a little girl ran in, pursued by a fair-haired, plump, and embarrassed maid.

'Look, Papa, look!' cried the child excitedly, holding something up for him to see. She noticed me, then, and her eyes became curious. She was clasping a newborn kitten in her hands. It was blind, and pathetically tiny, making faint, protesting squeaks.

'I'm sorry, sir.' The maid, crimson-faced, dropped a curtsey. 'We've some new kittens in the kitchen, and Miss Dorothy wanted to see them — '

'I wanted to show it to you, Papa,' finished the little girl.

She was thin and dark, and, I thought, rather drearily clad in a grey dress almost hidden under a brown holland pinafore.

'Dorothy, you must not burst into rooms like that,' said her father sternly. 'And you, Rosie, are supposed to be taking Miss Dorothy for walks, not encouraging her to spend her time in the kitchen,' he continued, addressing the blushing maid now.

'Yes, sir. I just thought she would like to see the kittens.'

'But look, Papa!' cried the child, holding the kitten up again. 'You look,' she said, suddenly turning to me. I reached out, and touched the tiny, groping head.

'Its mother will be looking for it,' I said.

'Will she?' Bright, dark eyes regarded me sharply out of a heart-shaped face.

'Yes,' said her father. 'You've shown us the kitten, Dorothy, and it's very pretty. But as Miss Mountjoy says, its mother will be looking for it. Take it back.'

The child glanced uncertainly from her father to me. Then, with a little giggle, she left the room as abruptly as she had come, with the flustered maid hurrying after her.

'As you have probably realised, that is my daughter,' said Mr. Tregarth. 'Since we have come to live here, she has had no proper discipline up to now. But I do not wish to discuss things fully today, as time is pressing. I shall ring for the dogcart now, and tomorrow morning it will bring you here.'

He rang the bell, remarking that if my references were satisfactory, he would like me to commence duties as Dorothy's governess as soon as possible. I felt both elated and apprehensive about things. Would my references be satisfactory, and if they were, what would it be like to be an employee at Abinger Hall? These thoughts ran through my mind as I once more sat in the hall, this time waiting for the dogcart.

While I was sitting there, a young

lady came slowly and gracefully down the stairs. She was extremely attractive, fair-haired, and tall. She glanced at me, and then glanced away again, as if I had not been there, and proceeded in the same direction that I had just come from.

I could feel myself flushing at the way in which she had totally ignored my presence. I remembered the waggoner's wife, and the gossip she had regaled me with. She had said the Squire was without a wife. Who then was the fair, haughty looking young lady who had passed so close to me, without the slightest sign of acknowledgement? Well, if I came to work at Abinger Hall I would soon find out.

A few minutes later I climbed into the Squire's dogcart. A ruddy-faced young man was driving it. We bowled along the drive and out of the gates at a smart pace. Back at the mill-house, I made myself a hurried meal, and with Barnaby at my heels, I went along to see Old Mollie again.

'Well, my lovely?'

'Mollie, I've been driven all the way back in the Squire's dogcart!'

'Ah! What did he say, then?'

'I might get a position there as his daughter's governess,' I said triumphantly.

'His daughter's governess! Why, 'ee couldn't do better! But what about the mill-house?'

'He's still going to put a miller in. But he says he'll get a cottage in the village done up for me, and that I needn't worry about things. He's sending the dogcart for me tomorrow, to take me to the Hall again.'

'Well, tell me everything, my love,' said Mollie, and I sat down and proceeded to do so.

The following morning I rose early, and was ready for the dogcart long before it came. It was another bright, sunny day, and after the gloom and unhappiness of the past few weeks, my spirits rose amazingly as the chestnut horse clip-clopped along the winding lanes, while the driver whistled cheerfully to himself. Again the footman answered the door to me at Abinger Hall, but this time his manner had changed somewhat.

'Miss Mountjoy . . . wait here one moment. I believe you are expected.'

I noticed that the flowers had been changed in the vases on the long oak table in the hall. There were visiting cards in a silver salver on it. The footman beckoned me to follow him, and once again I entered the library. Howard Tregarth greeted me, and after I was seated, he asked if he might see my references. I handed him them, and he read them through very carefully.

'Well, they seem satisfactory enough,' he remarked. 'My daughter is eight years old. She has been without a mother for nearly a year now, and has lived in Italy for most of her life.'

I wondered if I should say I was sorry about her motherless state, but somehow it seemed too familiar. Besides, Mr. Tregarth had spoken in a very matter-of-fact voice. I merely inclined my head.

'I have a young lady here who acts as my hostess,' he went on. 'For many years an old friend of my late uncle shared part of the house with him. This friend was a retired colonel — Colonel Hepton. The colonel had his own apartments in the house here, and attended to a number of my uncle's affairs. My uncle outlived the colonel by only a few months. Miss Hepton, the colonel's daughter, grew up here. Naturally, when I inherited the estate, I could scarcely change these arrangements immediately, so this lady is still here. She keeps an eye on my daughter, so to speak, but she has many other tasks to attend to. One of the maids looks after Dorothy, but it is not an ideal arrangement. The child needs a governess, and a few hours in the schoolroom every day. She needs someone to answer her questions intelligently, and teach her something.'

'She seems a very bright little girl,' I ventured.

'Perhaps. But up to now she has not done very well, largely due I think to the poor governesses she had in Italy. She cannot read yet.'

'Neither could one of the girls belonging to the family I was with in Plymouth,' I said. 'She was nearly eight years old. But she was reading well enough in a few months.'

He appeared to be impressed. 'I think we can consider the matter settled, then, Miss Mountjoy. You will, of course, be living here. It would not be convenient to send the dogcart to the mill-house every day, and you could not walk. Naturally, you will have some free time, and concerning your salary, I will give you a bit more than you received at your post in Plymouth, and as soon as Dorothy is reading fairly well, I shall be pleased to increase it.'

'Thank you, sir.'

He rang the bell, and when a housemaid appeared at the door, he asked for Miss Hepton to come to the library. 'I should like you to meet Miss Hepton as soon as possible,' he said. 'She will show you the nursery and schoolroom, and — er — discuss sleeping arrangements with you.'

'Shall I have meals with your daughter?' I asked, as he had not mentioned it.

'Breakfast and luncheon with her in the nursery, but she dines with us in the evenings.'

Two questions rose in my mind. Who was 'us,' and would I dine alone in the nursery? He answered that in the next breath.

'You would also be required to dine with us on most occasions. I have not done much entertaining as yet, but naturally, when we have guests, I would not wish my daughter to be present.'

Nor I, I thought.

'You do not, of course, ride?'

'I'm afraid not, sir.' I did not think he expected me to say that I did; after all, he had been surprised enough to find that I could speak French and play the piano.

'My daughter has not had any riding lessons yet, either. I think she would like to ride, but she seems a bit afraid of horses. I sometimes think it is because of a carriage accident — ah, Miss Hepton!'

The door was simultaneously rapped on and opened, and the tall, fair girl who had passed me so disdainfully in the hall the day before, entered the room. She smiled straight across at Mr. Tregarth.

'Miss Hepton, this is Miss Clare Mountjoy, and I have just engaged her services as governess for Dorothy. This is Miss Celia Hepton.'

The smile on her face wavered just a little as she looked at me. I felt she was sizing me up from head to toe in one cool glance.

'Good day to you,' she said, glancing back at him almost immediately. 'I was not aware that you had advertised the post, Howard.'

'I haven't. It's quite by chance. Miss Mountjoy called yesterday on a matter concerning the house she is in, and I discovered she is a governess looking for a post.'

'Most providential,' remarked Miss Hepton.

'Yes. Miss Mountjoy is to start as soon as possible, so I would be obliged if you would show her the nursery and schoolroom. She has met Dorothy, very briefly. She will be living here, as it is not practicable for her to travel every day to and from the village — besides, Dorothy needs her company as much as possible.' He glanced at the ormolu clock on the mantelshelf. 'You might show Miss Mountjoy round, and she had better stay to luncheon. It will not be long now before it is served.'

'You mean — luncheon with us?' she asked. I could feel myself flushing to the roots of my hair.

'Yes, I do mean luncheon with us,' was the reply, delivered in a very decisive tone of voice. In silence I followed Miss Hepton out of the library. I noticed she had coloured up, too.

'You live in the village, then?' was her opening remark.

'Yes, in the mill-house. Mr. Tregarth wants to get the mill working again, and put a miller in, so he wants me to vacate the house after the harvest,' I explained. 'I've just recently lost my grandmother, so I am alone there now.'

'I see. And you are a governess?' There was just enough surprise in her voice to make the question faintly insulting. Miss Hepton led me up the splendid, carved staircase.

'I too have suffered bereavement,' she said. 'I have lived here for many years with my father. We shared Abinger Hall with old Mr. Tregarth, and then my father died, and shortly afterwards Uncle Lionel, as I called him. Abinger Hall is home to me, a fact which his nephew understands, of course. I have my own apartments here; I still carry on with the tasks which I was accustomed to perform when my father and Mr. Tregarth were alive.'

It was plain that she didn't wish me to think she was in anything like the same circumstances as I was.

'The drawing room,' she said, not without pride. It was certainly a beautiful room. A great crystal chandelier hung from an exquisitely carved ceiling, and there were gilt chairs, and a grand piano. At first I thought the room even larger than it was, as there was an enormous mirror fitted into one wall, reflecting the windows and giving an illusion of still more light and space.

'This is an Adam fireplace,' said Miss Hepton.

'It's very impressive,' I said. I looked at the pictures on the walls, and at the figurines, and glass display cases full of delicate pieces of china.

'All the woodwork was carved by Italians, and the ceilings too,' Miss Hepton informed me. 'Mr. Tregarth has had this room redecorated, and any necessary repairs done. Uncle Lionel just let everything go, and even Papa couldn't make him realise that the house needed constant upkeep. Well, he probably realised it, but he didn't care. Now, however, everything is being done. Mr. Tregarth has a tremendous task facing him, and of course, he has all the estate to think about, too. His uncle never bothered about that, either.'

'I think the villagers realize that,' I said. 'As you say, there must be a great deal to do.' She led me from room to room, talking about Abinger Hall all the time. Repairs and decorating were going on in various places; ladders and paint tins and buckets appeared in different rooms. She showed me the nursery. It was a shabby room, with worn linoleum covering the floor. There was a well worn rocking horse, and various dolls strewn around. I noticed there were new curtains up at the window, as if some attempt had been made to brighten up the place for Howard Tregarth's daughter.

There was a coal fire, and a large

fireguard in front of it.

'Dorothy will be out walking with the maid, I expect,' said Miss Hepton. 'This is the schoolroom.' The adjoining room on one side was even more dreary. There were two scratched and battered desks, and a table and blackboard. There were several stools and chairs around, and a number of large cupboards. It smelled musty, and I had a feeling it was a long time since anyone had been taught there.

'I had a governess when I was small,' explained my guide. 'I was the last child to be taught here, but the last Tregarth to be taught here was Uncle Lionel's son. I went away to school, and only came back for holidays, but when I was sixteen I came back for good. This other door leading off from the nursery is where Dorothy sleeps.'

I was shown into a bedroom containing two single beds, and a child's cot. There was also an oak dressing-table and a wardrobe, a hip bath, and a marble washstand and basin.

'The maid is sleeping here with her at the moment,' said Miss Hepton. 'I suppose you would not object to sharing this room with Dorothy until a room is ready for you?'

'Not at all. Where would my room be?'

'I think this room across the corridor would be the most suitable.' We left the nursery, and taking a key from the bunch she had with her, Miss Hepton unlocked the door of a room on the opposite side of the corridor to the night nursery. 'Although I was taught in the schoolroom, I never slept in this part of the house,' she remarked. 'I think it is a long time since this room was used.'

I glanced around. Everything was swathed in dust sheets, and it smelled cold and musty. It was certainly not inviting.

'When it is cleaned, and the bed prepared, and a fire lit, it will be somewhat different. You are not of a nervous disposition, are you?'

'Nervous?' I repeated. 'No, scarcely that. I live alone in the mill-house now.'

'The servants talk of ghosts and things,' she said, with a wry smile. 'No doubt you are well used to such chatter. I'll show you the servants' hall. I still have my private rooms here, of course. Old Mr. Tregarth saw no need to employ a separate housekeeper and cook, so the cook, Mrs. Stevens, acts as housekeeper as well. For the past few years, though, I've done a good deal of the actual household management at Abinger Hall, and, naturally, I act as hostess for Mr. Tregarth. It is all rather unorthodox, I suppose, but it seems to be an agreeable arrangement for all concerned. My days are very full.'

I met Mrs. Stevens, and some of the housemaids. I could see that my position at Abinger Hall was going to be more clearly defined than that of Miss Hepton. I knew exactly the category which a governess fell into. I was not one of the servants, but I was still paid for my services. Miss Hepton glanced at her gold watch.

'It will soon be luncheon,' she remarked. 'We have it served in the morning room. As a rule, there is just myself and Mr. Tregarth. In the evening, though, he insists on the presence of his daughter at the dinner table.'

'He mentioned that to me,' I said. 'He also said that he would expect me to dine downstairs in the evening, too.'

'I see.' There was a slight pause before Miss Hepton spoke. She did not say anything further, but I sensed that this arrangement did not please her. Shortly afterwards we were summoned to luncheon. The morning room was spacious and charming, and bore signs of having been recently decorated. A stony-faced butler, Mathers, waited at table, assisted by the footman.

I was overcome by shyness. The table was beautifully laid, although there were only three of us at luncheon. I was not accustomed to drinking wine with my meals, but I had a glass, rather than refuse that awe inspiring butler. We had soup, game pie, and vegetables. A delicious pudding was served, after which Miss Hepton poured the coffee for us.

During the meal, she and Mr. Tregarth had talked almost continuously about what needed doing in the house, although he had drawn me into the conversation several times. He asked if I had seen the nursery, and which room Miss Hepton thought most suitable for me. She told him the one opposite the night nursery.

'The Blue Room,' he said. 'I believe that is what the servants call it.'

'It's all rather faded now, I'm afraid.' Miss Hepton handed me a cup of coffee. 'Very musty smelling, and covered in dust sheets. But with some organisation it can soon be put to rights. Meanwhile, I thought Miss Mountjoy could take Rosie's place in Dorothy's bedroom.'

'If Miss Mountjoy is agreeable.' Howard Tregarth looked at me enquiringly. I said that I was. 'Then you seem to have arranged things to everyone's satisfaction,' he said to Miss Hepton. He turned to me again.

'We are very busy with repairs and decorations here, as no doubt you have been told, Miss Mountjoy.'

'I have indeed, and I can see what a big task it is,' I replied.

Before I left in the dogcart, it was agreed that I should be ready to begin my duties one week later, when the dogcart would call for me again. This time a much older man drove me back. He was white-haired and his shoulders were bowed, but his eyes were still bright in his weather-beaten face. He told me his name was Will Pyke.

'Is it true you be coming here to be governess to Miss Dorothy?' he asked.

'Yes,' I replied, with a smile. 'Have you worked at Abinger Hall long?'

'Fifty-five years, man and boy,' was the reply. 'I'm the head coachman. And you be wanting to go to the mill-house?'

'Yes, please.' For some time he drove

along in silence.

'You will know the Tregarth family very well, then?' I began again.

'All my life. I'm hopeful, now, miss, that things will be as they once were. When the old Squire was young, and his wife was alive, and Master Anthony a child, Abinger Hall was a fine place to be in. They held the Hunt Ball there, with the best in the county coming. Ah, the carriages that used to drive up to the house! And the harvest supper, with all the village there, and the fiddlers playing. There would be a whole roast ox, and dancing and laughter until morning . . . ' He shook his head at the memory, and fell silent again.

'Did the old Squire's wife die when she was young, then?' I asked. I had never been very interested in what had happened at the Hall before now. I had known from childhood that the Squire lived there, but that he never appeared in public much, and certainly never came anywhere near the village.

'Yes, and he never got over that,

rightly. But there were other troubles.'

'You must have liked working for him,' I remarked.

'Every man has his faults. And life do change people. It isn't only poor folks has heavy crosses to bear. Whatever I was asked to do, I would have done. And now young Mr. Tregarth is starting off with his share of troubles, too.' He shook his head, and clucked to the horse.

'He's old Mr. Tregarth's nephew, isn't he?'

'Great-nephew, miss. Life's all chance, all chance. And here he is, with everything in a fine mess, and he's got a child to bring up, too. And the colonel's daughter's still here, too.'

Later that day I confided all my news in Mollie. As Barnaby was a regular visitor to her cottage, she had no objection to caring for him all the time. It would be a wrench leaving him, but I knew that he was in good hands.

'I'll be along to see the mill-house is all right,' Mollie promised. 'It were a blessing you went to see the young Squire after all.'

The next few days found me busy. One of my problems was how to improve my wardrobe. I had enough clothes for everyday wear, although they were all very plain. It was the thought of dining every evening with the Squire and Miss Hepton which filled me with dread. What would I wear? I had nothing suitable. In despair I told Old Mollie.

'Well,' she said slowly. 'I do keep a trunk of clothes under the bed — things folks have given me from time to time. Help me pull it out.'

In the cramped disorder of Mollie's bedroom, I helped her drag the trunk out. The room seemed to be full of boxes and rubbish, rather as if she had just moved in, when, in fact, she had lived there for years. She opened the lid of the trunk, and a jumbled mass of clothes was revealed.

'Folks have many a time given me things,' she explained. 'Something might be of use, my love.' I doubted it; the villagers had little enough to give, and the trunk appeared to contain but a motley set of rags and pieces.

'Have 'ee got a black skirt?' asked Mollie, holding up a piece of really pretty blue silk. 'There be enough here to make a blouse, and that would be suitable evening wear for a governess, surely?'

'Yes, I think you're right,' I said.

'And look, here's some lace.' She held up a length of fine, crocheted white lace. 'You could make another blouse out of this. I don't think there's much else of use. But I can help with the sewing.'

'Thank you, Mollie. Two new blouses will be a great help,' I said.

'I still can't get used to the idea that you be going to teach the Squire's daughter,' she went on. 'It was new moon the day you went, I know. Your luck changed with a waxing moon, it seems.'

'I've been very lucky,' I agreed. My

chances of finding a situation so close to Bramwell were not very good. True, Abinger Hall was not the only large house in the vicinity. The market town of Chollerford was several miles from Bramwell, and there were two or three houses near there as big, if not bigger than the Squire's residence. My mother had been a governess in one of them. I had been buying copies of the Chollerford Weekly Journal in the hope that someone in the district would be advertising for a governess. And now, out of the blue, I had obtained such a situation.

With Mollie's help I made two evening blouses. When they were finished she stood in the bedroom at the mill-house, and watched me try them both on.

'Well, I don't know which you look the prettiest in, my love. You look like a duchess in them both, and that's the truth of it.'

There was a peculiar expression on Mollie's face.

'What's wrong?' I asked. 'Don't you like my hair done like this?' I had dressed it high on my head.

'It looks lovely. You'll not shame the Squire when you dine with him.'

Barnaby padded into the room.

'You're coming to live with me, my beauty,' said Mollie.

'I hope he doesn't fret,' I said. 'I know he'll miss me. I shall miss him, and you, Mollie. But I shall be back to see you as soon as possible.'

3

'This is my best doll,' said Dorothy. 'I want to play with her a lot, but she's so special I'm afraid of breaking her.' We were in the nursery together, and Dorothy was showing me her toys. They were a motley selection of dolls and picture books. She was excited at having me there, and I realized she was bored, in spite of the companionship of the young maid, and, to a certain extent, that of Miss Hepton.

'We shall have to buy you some better books,' I remarked. I'll read you some stories now.'

'Rosie doesn't read me stories, but she tells me them. She frightens me sometimes.'

'Does she indeed?' I was not really surprised to hear that. Rosie seemed a good-natured girl, but I could imagine some of the stories she had told

Dorothy. Old Mollie had a good supply of such tales, which my mother and grandmother had always told me not to take any notice of. One such tale was about a certain number of people drowning in the river each year. She used to say that every river took it's own share of lives, and that our river, the Sedge, which widened and deepened further along, took three. I knew her own husband had been drowned in it, and I sometimes wondered how she could bear to go on living beside it afterwards.

'Look at my doll, Miss Mountjoy,' said Dorothy. 'She's called Violet.'

It was a wax doll with yellow curls and blue eyes which opened and closed. It was dressed in pink silk.

'Who bought her for you?'

'Papa. Before we came to England. He said I could have any doll I wanted as soon as I could read, so I pretended I could.'

'But that was very naughty if you couldn't.'

'Yes.' Dorothy giggled. 'I learnt to say the same piece over and over again. Miss Jones, my governess, helped me.'

'And what happened?' I asked.

'Papa came into the nursery, and heard me read out of my book. I had learnt every page. He was pleased, and I got my doll.'

I had no doubt that Miss Jones had received an increase in salary for her part in the deception.

'But later on Papa bought me a book, and asked me to read from it. I couldn't, and he was very cross. Miss Jones had to go. He told me that I hadn't really deserved Violet, but he wouldn't take her away, because it wasn't all my fault.'

'You will soon learn to read,' I told her. 'We'll get some really nice books.'

'I only had one English governess, and that was Miss Jones,' said Dorothy. 'The others were Italian. They used to read to me in Italian.'

She didn't say anything more about her life in Italy, and although I would have liked to hear more, I did not press her.

It was my first day at Abinger Hall, and I was finding it very interesting. The room across the corridor from the nursery was being prepared for me, and meanwhile I was sharing Dorothy's room.

'Won't you sleep with me always?' she asked. 'I'm afraid of the dark.'

'You're not in the dark, Dorothy, you have a nightlight. When I move into the other room, you can always come to me if you wake in the night.'

'But that room . . . Rosie says it's haunted, Miss Mountjoy.'

'Haunted?' I thought then of what Miss Hepton had said about the servants talking about ghosts, when she had first shown me the room.

'Then she has no right to tell you such nonsense,' I said briskly. 'Forget all about that, Dorothy. We'll put on our outdoor clothes, and go for a walk before luncheon. We'll look for all the wild flowers blooming at this time of the year. And you can show me the grounds.'

I had plaited her straight, dark hair into two neat braids, tied with ribbon. It gave her a much more cared for appearance, although she had not liked the idea at first.

'When we go anywhere special, and when your papa takes you out, you can wear it loose,' I promised her. 'And it won't be straight, then. It will have little waves in it.' She seemed greatly taken with this idea.

What unattractive clothes the child was wearing, though. She had grown out of most of them, too. She was still more or less in mourning, and the blacks and greys ill became her colouring.

I put on my own hastily dyed black cloak with a feeling of distaste. Remembering my grandmother's wishes, I resolved to get out of mourning myself as soon as possible. We looked a dreary enough pair as we walked down the steps and onto the terrace that morning. It was a blustery kind of spring day, less warm than it had been, with a hint of rain on the wind. I held Dorothy's hand, while she prattled away, showing me this and that, and obviously enjoying herself. There were several dogs at Abinger Hall, I learnt, but they were all kept in the stables and the kitchen. One, a setter called Twinkle, accompanied us on our walk.

'Papa doesn't mind dogs,' said Dorothy. 'But he likes them kept away from our rooms.'

'I have a dog called Barnaby,' I told her. 'But I've had to leave him behind.'

'Who's looking after him?'

'Someone we call Old Mollie. She lives in a cottage close to the mill-house. He is quite happy with her.'

'Bring him here. Papa wouldn't mind.'

I laughed. 'No, I think he is better where he is.' Dorothy wanted to know all about the mill-house. She was fascinated by the idea of living beside the river.

'It's much nicer living here,' I said, glancing around.

'Would you like to see the stables?' asked Dorothy. 'Can you ride?'

'No.'

'Neither can I. Aunt Celia rides a lot, though. She and Papa ride together.'

So that was what she called Miss Hepton. And she and Howard Tregarth rode together . . .

The stables were quite big, and there was a carriage house. I saw that there was a brougham, as well as the dogcart. Will Pyke was sitting on an upturned box, smoking a pungent smelling pipe. When he saw me with Dorothy he gave a knowing grin.

'You be learning your lessons, Miss Dorothy?' he asked. 'Or be you here to learn to ride? Your papa is out riding now, with Miss Hepton.'

'I don't want to learn to ride,' said Dorothy loudly. 'Anyway, the stable smells.'

Taking my hand, she hurried out, and across the cobbled stableyard. I guessed that in her heart she wanted to learn to ride, but was somewhat nervous of the actual process of learning.

'Now I'll show you where the old quarry is,' she announced.

'Quarry? I didn't know there was a quarry in the grounds,' I said.

'There used to be, long, long ago, Papa said. But it's fenced off, with trees round it. Come on, I'll show you.'

She ran along in front, slipping on the damp grass as she ascended a slope. I could see rotting fencing, and some bushes.

'Come on, Miss Mountjoy!'

I hurried after my lively charge, and joined her, standing on the brink of a great, yawning, yellow-grey gash in the earth.

'Come on, let's go down,' said Dorothy.

'No, you're not to,' I said sharply. 'It's steep, and it's very muddy down there.' Twinkle, who had left us once to romp around the stables, had caught us up again, and ran round the circumference of the quarry, barking wildly.

'Rosie lets me go down.' Dorothy's voice was rebellious.

'I am not Rosie,' I explained patiently. 'There's nothing to go down there for, and anyway, if luncheon is served at one o'clock, we should be back in the house shortly.'

'I haven't shown you half yet.'

'Never mind, there is plenty of time for you to do that.'

'Will you race me back, then?'

'Very well. I'll race you as far as that big oak tree.'

'How do you know it's an oak tree?'

'Because of the shape of it. You must learn all that, Dorothy.'

She began to run, followed by the barking Twinkle. I ran after her, and while we were thus engaged, I noticed two horsemen approaching from another part of the grounds. They were not two men, though, I soon realised. I could see the splash of a bright blue riding habit, and I guessed it was Mr. Tregarth and Miss Hepton returning to the house after their ride. They would see us, too, and I wondered what Dorothy's father would think when he saw us both scampering along.

We arrived back in the house, warm and breathless, and in good spirits. Dorothy announced that she had won. Back in the shabby nursery, an excellent luncheon was served by the parlourmaid. A spotless cloth was laid on the deal table, and a tray with a tureen and plates was brought in.

'This is nice,' said Dorothy, after the maid had gone. 'I used to have meals alone, before you came, except for dinner. Rosie used to stand and talk to me while I ate. One of the grooms is Rosie's sweetheart. She told me.'

It was plain to me that Dorothy had heard far too much of servants' gossip.

'You must have spent some of your time with Miss Hepton,' I said.

'Aunt Celia? Sometimes in the afternoons she takes me to her sitting room, and plays the piano for me.'

'And do you like that?' I asked, giving her some more vegetables.

'Yes. I used to dance round the room while she was playing. Can you dance? I mean properly, like people do at balls?'

'Well, yes, I suppose I can.' At Plymouth, the two elder daughters of the Thomas family had received dancing lessons at the house, and hearing I could not dance, their mother had suggested I should join them for tuition. I told Dorothy about this, and she was most interested.

'I can play the piano for you, now I'm here,' I said. 'I have a song book with me, and I can teach you songs, too.'

'Papa spends a lot of time in the library,' she said, a little wistfully. 'Nobody goes in the drawing room in the afternoons. We could play the piano, and we could have tea there, too.'

'We will, then, if nobody minds. You are old enough to start learning the piano yourself.'

After luncheon it began to rain, and I sat and read to Dorothy, and encouraged her to ask questions afterwards.

Then we went downstairs, and she led me into the newly decorated drawing room.

'Now you stand up and I'll sit, and you can put your fingers on the notes after me,' I said. 'I'll show you your five finger exercises. Watch carefully.' She was quite interested, and very pleased when I guided her own small hands onto the keys.

'Let me do it! Let me do it!' she cried. I let her sit on the piano stool and practise with one hand. I did not hear the door open, and Howard Tregarth's voice made me jump.

'So here you are — both of you!'

'Listen, Papa!' cried Dorothy.

'Yes, very good, to be sure.' He was smiling, and suddenly looked very boyish.

'You are settling down without any problems, then, Miss Mountjoy?' he asked.

'Yes, sir, I think so. There are one or two things concerning Dorothy's education which I would like to discuss with you.'

'Is there anything particularly pressing?'

'Well, sir, I would like her to have some new books, and one or two other things for the schoolroom.'

'Certainly. She can have anything you think necessary. Is it possible to buy what you need in Chollerford?'

'Most things, I think.'

'In that case, we will have an expedition there.'

Dorothy stopped practising. 'Have a what, Papa?'

'An expedition to Chollerford, to buy books and things for you.'

'What's an expedition?'

'Ask Miss Mountjoy. Your hair looks very nice.'

'Miss Mountjoy says it looks tidier but if you take me out, she says I can wear it loose again, and it will be all little waves. I expect hers is like that when she takes it down.' Her artless chatter embarrassed me; there was no knowing what she might say next.

'I saw you going for a walk this

morning, or perhaps I should say run,' remarked her father.

'Yes, I raced Miss Mountjoy. She wouldn't let me go down into the quarry.'

'I should think not.' Her father gave me an approving glance. 'I'm afraid she's rather a tomboy.'

'She has plenty of energy, sir. Fortunately, I have as well.'

'Dance with me, Papa!' cried Dorothy. 'Miss Mountjoy will play for us. Please.'

'You can't dance yet.'

'But Miss Mountjoy is going to teach me! She learnt when she was a governess at another house. They used to have lessons every Wednesday afternoon, and they all used to join in, and have tea afterwards. She told me.'

'Well, if Miss Mountjoy is accustomed to such things — ' he gave an indulgent smile. 'Come on, then. On the polished floor, not on the carpet.'

'I'll play a waltz,' I said. A shaft of sunlight broke through a thread of blue sky, and lit up the room where Dorothy and her father stood, I began to play, and I could see him trying to guide her little feet along. There was something strangely touching about the two of them dancing together like that.

'Now you dance with Miss Mountjoy,' was Dorothy's next suggestion.

'You can't play yet, Dorothy, and we must have music,' he said quickly, realizing how embarrassed I was.

'Aunt Celia can play, though.'

'Aunt Celia is out visiting this afternoon. Isn't it time for tea now?'

'We're having it in here, not in the nursery. Miss Mountjoy says we can.'

'As I had promised to start teaching her the piano — I thought — ' I began haltingly.

'Very well. We'll all have it in here together.'

The way Dorothy kept quoting what I said, it sounded as if I were having a lot to say about everything. Her father told her to ring for the tea to be brought, and we took it sitting beside the fire. At Mr. Tregarth's request, I poured the tea from the graceful silver teapot, and handed round wafer thin bread and butter, tiny scones, and seed cake.

'Isn't this nice?' asked Dorothy, munching heartily. 'What are you looking at, Miss Mountjoy?'

'I'm just looking at some of the portraits on the wall,' I replied.

'I don't know who they are,' said Dorothy. 'Do you, Papa?'

'Not all of them. But I can find out from the library if I want to.'

'Well, who's that?' Dorothy pointed to a portrait of a man with a somewhat stern cast of feature.

'My great-uncle Lionel.'

'And that?' She pointed to a painting of a dark young woman in a low-cut dress.

'That was my Aunt Alice, my uncle's wife.'

'She has a nose like Miss Mountjoy.'

'Really, Dorothy, you shouldn't make remarks about people's noses. You have a very long tongue,' said her father severely.

'Why is it long? How do you know it is long?' Dorothy was unable to fathom this out. She stuck out a crumb-coated tongue, and we were both scolding her when the door opened, and Miss Hepton stood there in her outdoor clothes. She looked rather annoyed.

'Why, Celia, I thought you were visiting at the Grimthorpes',' said Mr. Tregarth, rising, and looking surprised.

'The road there is blocked by an overturned waggon,' she said crossly. 'They were waiting for help to get it up. I told Pyke to turn back. I shall have to write and apologize. It's too tiresome. And it's a perfectly horrid afternoon, raining, and quite cold.'

'Never mind. Come and join us round the fire, and I'll ring for more tea,' said Mr. Tregarth. 'Miss Mountjoy has been giving Dorothy a music lesson, and we have all ended up having tea here.'

'How very nice.' Miss Hepton advanced

towards the fire, and drew off her gloves. She was wearing a dark, grey-blue, fur-trimmed coat, with a matching bonnet. It suited her fair colouring very well, and the fact that she was flushed with annoyance enhanced her attractiveness. I felt nondescript and shabby beside her. The maid supplied more tea, and Miss Hepton began to look more mollified.

'Where was the waggon overturned?' asked Mr. Tregarth, while Dorothy listened eagerly. She was always avid for any morsel of gossip. She could not sit still for long, though, and having eaten her tea, she went off to the piano again, and tried to find middle C, without success.

'Dorothy!' called her father. Miss Hepton shot me a baleful glance, which left me in no doubt what to do.

'Please excuse me. I must take Dorothy back to the nursery,' I said, rising and walking towards my charge.

'I shall see you at dinner, Papa!' she shouted, as we left the room. She was a handful, there was no doubt about that.

Back in the nursery I read picture books to her until it was time to change for dinner. When Dorothy was ready I attended to my own toilet, putting on the blue silk blouse.

'That's pretty,' said the child admiringly. 'Have you any pearls? Aunt Celia wears pearls.'

My heart sank a little. I had no pearls, no jewellery of any kind. But then, why should I mind? I could never hope to compete with Miss Hepton, and there was no reason why I should want to. In spite of telling myself this, though, I heartily wished that I was not required to go down to dinner with Dorothy. She herself was quite excited by the idea, and danced along in front of me, down the stairs and along the corridors.

I had never been inside such a large house in my life, although I knew that it was smaller than Tyzanger Grange; smaller, probably, than some of the other country houses round about. I had only had a brief glimpse of the dining room; it was impressively handsome, but in need of decorating. The four of us took our places at the large mahogany table.

Miss Hepton appeared to have recovered from her ill humour at having to turn back from her visit. She was dressed in black, and wearing a single row of pearls. It reminded me that she too was officially in mourning for her father, although she seemed to suit herself in this matter. I saw her eyes flicker over me as we sat down, and realized with a sudden shock that there was barely veiled hostility in them. Mr. Tregarth also looked at me; a look of approval, combined with slight surprise.

It gave me confidence; I remembered Mollie's words: 'You'll not shame the Squire when you dine with him'.

Dorothy was not allowed to chatter at the dinner table. She had told me this beforehand. It was an effort for her to keep so quiet, but she knew that if she didn't, she was liable to be banished to the nursery.

'I shall be going to Chollerford on Thursday, market day, this week to attend court there,' said Mr. Tregarth. 'Being a magistrate, I have to go there quite frequently. You and Dorothy can come with me, Miss Mountjoy, and you can buy anything you require there. If you can't get all you need, we will send away for it.'

'Thank you. There is a very good book shop there,' I said. 'I would also like to buy some silks and pieces of linen, so that Dorothy can learn to embroider.'

'You have a free hand,' he said blandly.

'Oh, really, Howard, do you have to go to Chollerford on market day?' Miss Hepton's voice was peevish.

Howard Tregarth raised his eyebrows. 'I'm afraid I do. I was not aware that there was anything of importance to prevent me.'

'Mrs. Boldwood asked me if we could ride over there one morning this week, and she said the most convenient day for her would be Thursday.'

'I see. But this was not an official invitation, I gather?'

'Well, no. It's nothing formal; she just mentioned it.'

'And you did not think it worth while mentioning it to me before now? You took it for granted I would come?'

I felt extremely embarrassed. It was obvious that Mr. Tregarth was annoyed at Miss Hepton accepting an invitation on his behalf. She changed her attitude quickly at the tone of his voice.

'As it was not an official invitation, Howard, it does not matter.' Her voice was placating; she smiled winningly at Howard Tregarth. Above the softly curving mouth, though, her blue eyes looked at me with venom.

'Ride there yourself, Celia; we can go together another day,' he said. 'I'm sure Mrs. Boldwood will understand, if you give her my apologies.'

I was already forming certain opinions about Miss Hepton. I imagined Mr. Tregarth had been put in a rather awkward position concerning her, when he had inherited the house. After all, it had been her home for many years; he could hardly ask her to leave the moment he walked in. *She* was no mill-house tenant, I thought bitterly. I had not seen the rooms she occupied at Abinger Hall. She did not appear to have her meals in them, anyway. The dinner was excellent. There was wine on the table, but I drank only water. Although the food was so good, I still did not feel altogether at ease dining there. I supposed if Mr. Tregarth was busy during the day, allowing Dorothy to join him for dinner ensured that he would see her then, if at no other time. He and Miss Hepton talked amicably enough throughout the remainder of the meal.

'Papa, may I play my card game with you in the library tonight?' asked Dorothy when it was over.

'Not tonight, I'm afraid. I'm seeing a gentleman about something.'

Dorothy had told me that she usually spent some time with her father after dinner. She looked very disappointed.

'Miss Mountjoy will play with you in the nursery,' he said consolingly. 'She needs you to keep her company on her first evening here. You can say your goodnights now.'

Accordingly, we both said them and Miss Hepton withdrew at the same time. I wondered how she was going to spend the evening. Presumably, as she had her own apartments, she could entertain whom she pleased. Perhaps she too was expecting a visitor. I did not think she was older than two and twenty, and it was most unusual for a girl of her class to have the freedom which she apparently had. Dorothy skipped on ahead of me, quite reconciled to the fact that she would not be spending any time with her father that evening. It was a wet, unpleasant night, but there was a cheerful fire in the nursery.

'When we first came here, I didn't use to go downstairs and have dinner with Papa.'

'It must be because he thinks you are growing up, Dorothy.'

'Rosie says it's because he doesn't want people to talk.'

'Talk? About what?'

'I don't know. That's all she said.'

'I think Rosie says far too much, Dorothy. Now let's play some games until bedtime.'

I kept thinking about what the maid had said to her, though. Evidently Mr. Tregarth did not wish to dine alone with Miss Hepton, so he had his daughter brought down in the evenings. He and Miss Hepton lunched together, apparently, but perhaps not every day. Did they breakfast together? I pulled myself up sharply, thinking that it was none of my business. It was a strange household, though.

I read to Dorothy, and played quiet games with her until it was her bedtime. She was still excited at having a governess.

'When will you come to bed? Are you going to read to yourself, now, Miss Mountjoy?'

'Yes, I expect I shall sit and read,' I said. 'I shan't be late to bed, Dorothy.' Under my supervision she had folded up her clothes, neatly. She said her prayers, and climbed into bed.

'When I wake up it will be funny to see you here instead of Rosie,' she said.

I thought it would be strange for me to wake up and find her sleeping in the other bed, instead of waking up to hear Barnaby breathing heavily close beside me. I changed into my nightgown and wrapper, and sat beside the nursery fire reading. It was all very quiet and still. It was all very strange, too, and I felt as if it had been a long day. Dorothy seemed to me to be an affectionate child, and she had taken to me straight away. I wondered if poor Barnaby was settling down with Mollie. He would be pining for me, I was sure of that.

At last I extinguished the lamp, and went into the night nursery, where I finally slipped into bed, in the shadowed dimness of the night light. Although I was tired, sleep was long in coming. Would I be happy here? Only time would tell. I did not think I would have any real difficulties with Dorothy, and her father seemed prepared to give me a free hand.

Even so, I felt uneasy. I knew that I had not imagined that icy stare across the dinner table. Celia Hepton resented and disliked me. I was sure of it.

4

I sat in the brougham with Dorothy and her father sitting together on the opposite seat. We were bowling smoothly along on our way to Chollerford. It was quite early in the morning, as Mr. Tregarth had to attend the court.

Dorothy was in high spirits at the prospect of a day out to buy new books and equipment for the schoolroom. It was market day, and we passed several waggons going in the same direction. It was bright and sunny, with the uncertain glory of a spring day, and this added to the pleasurable anticipation of our shopping. The meadows were not laid up for mowing yet; the sheep were still feeding in them, and their bleating mingled with the melody of the larks' song. The cow parsley was blooming in the hedgerows, and it seemed that all things were green and growing, and that the hard frosts of early spring were already a thing of the past.

'Miss Mountjoy says she wants to see a dressmaker, if we have time,' announced Dorothy. 'She wants to have a new costume made.' As happened so often, Dorothy's artless statement made me feel slightly embarrassed.

'Is there a good dressmaker in Chollerford?' enquired her father.

'There is one who is quite good,' I said.

He eyed the drab grey cloak Dorothy was wearing. 'I think it is time you had some new outfits, too, Dorothy. What do you think, Miss Mountjoy?'

I had not had the courage to mention this matter to him as yet, so I was relieved when he broached the subject first.

'I agree with you, sir. She has outgrown some of them, and I think she has been in mourning long enough for a little girl, if I may say so.'

'You may well be right,' he said, after a slight pause. 'Abinger Hall is rather full of people in mourning at the moment. He glanced at my black cloak and grey dress as he spoke. Yes, we were all in mourning, I reflected.

'I intend to come out of it as soon as possible,' I said. 'Not because of any disrespect for my grandmother, but because she requested me not to wear it for long.'

'You may replace Dorothy's wardrobe with more suitable clothes, too,' he said. 'I think you can be trusted to show good taste.'

'Thank you, sir,' I replied.

'May I have a white dress with a blue sash?' asked Dorothy straight away. 'And a tartan cloak, like one of my dolls has?'

'Miss Mountjoy will buy you what she considers is necessary and suitable,' said her father firmly. 'You may not have time today.'

'We will, won't we, Miss Mountjoy?'

'We'll try,' I said. We were approaching Chollerford now. On market days it was a bustling and busy place. The market square, with its ancient cross, was thronged with people jostling around the stalls, buying and selling. There was a corn exchange, and a cattle market. The driver took the brougham round the back of an inn called The Seven Stars. We all alighted from the carriage, Mr. Tregarth lifting Dorothy down, while she squealed with delight. He offered me his hand as I descended the steps. I still felt slightly ill at ease in his presence. It was always something of an ordeal for me in the evenings, when I would dress myself and Dorothy, and join him and Miss Hepton in the sombre splendour of the dining room. He took out his gold watch, and looked at it.

'I have an hour before I attend court. Simkins can accompany us, and carry any parcels back to the carriage. We will see about the books first.'

The footman, Simkins, had been sitting with the driver. He followed us as we walked up the high street. It was full of countrywomen in bonnets and shawls, accompanied by rosy-cheeked children, laughing and shouting. Some of the women had come to Chollerford for the day out, and could afford to buy little enough. Others had come with their menfolk, who would be selling various wares in the market, while their wives and children looked around. I stopped outside a shop called Markham and Son, Stationers, Booksellers.

'I think we may find some suitable books here, sir,' I said. We entered the shop, which had a faint smell of dust and newly-bound books. An old man, and a middle-aged one, obviously father and son, rushed forward to greet us when we entered the shop, and I was offered a chair straight away. With an air of quiet authority, Mr. Tregarth explained that we were looking for suitable reading books and other schoolroom requisites for a child.

'We have a good supply of such things, sir,' said Mr. Markham senior, eagerly, stroking his enormous grey beard, which I could see was intriguing

Dorothy. Soon we were absorbed in looking at reading books, geography books, history books, maps, rulers, and pencils.

'And we have water colours and brushes if the young lady likes painting,' said the younger Mr. Markham, smiling at Dorothy.

'I think she should have a colour-box, sir,' I said to Mr. Tregarth. He seemed quite content to leave the choosing of everything to me. His daughter's interest in our purchases clearly pleased him. Pink with excitement, she watched the pile of books on the counter grow larger.

'I think there is plenty here for Dorothy to be going on with for the time being, sir,' I said.

'We can always order books for you — anything you want, we can get for you,' said Mr. Markham senior.

'Thank you. We will probably be needing more books later on,' replied Howard Tregarth. He consulted his watch again. 'If you will parcel these up, we can take them with us now.'

'I can't read yet,' announced Dorothy loudly. 'But I'm going to learn to read. And I'm going to write my name on all these books. Dorothy Tregarth.'

At the name Tregarth, both men appeared interested.

'Well, if you are a Miss Tregarth from Abinger Hall, by any chance,' said the older one, 'then we have supplied books for the schoolroom there before now. But it was a long time ago.' He beamed at Dorothy.

'Yes, we are from Abinger Hall,' said her father. The footman took charge of a large parcel, and the two men bowed us politely out of the shop.

'Look, there's a toy shop,' exclaimed Dorothy.

'You don't require any toys,' said her father. Then he turned to me. 'There is nothing she requires, is there?'

'Well, sir,' I said boldly. 'Dorothy is a very active child, and I think a skipping rope would give her a good deal of pleasure, as well as exercise. Also, she only has an old playing ball, which she found in the nursery. I think she might have a new one.'

'What's that thing with feathers on?' asked Dorothy, her face pressed to the thick glass panes of the window.

'That's a shuttlecock,' I explained. 'You play shuttlecock and battledore with it.'

'Papa! May I have one?' Her father's usually serious grey eyes met mine, and there was a decided twinkle in them.

'It seems I am outnumbered,' he said, and we went inside the shop, emerging some time later with a parcel containing a skipping rope, shuttlecock, a ball, and sundry other small items. Simkins was still in attendance, and now, loaded up, he was going to put everything in the carriage.

'I shall have to leave you soon,' said Mr. Tregarth. 'Where is the dressmaker, Miss Mountjoy?'

'Not far away. Just round the corner,' I said. He looked somewhat dubious.

'I usually have luncheon at The

Seven Stars when I attend court,' he said. 'It is not, of course, suitable for you and Dorothy. Do you know of somewhere in Chollerford where it is?'

'Yes, I do know of a very respectable place where they serve luncheons on market days. It is very quiet there.'

'Where is it?'

'It's in a street called Byner Street. The café is called Green Trees.'

He turned to Simkins. 'Take the parcels and put them in the carriage as soon as possible. I will walk to the Town Hall with Miss Mountjoy and Miss Dorothy, and I want you to be there as soon as you can, to accompany them wherever else they go in the town. I also want you to go with them to the Green Trees café, and reserve a table there for one o'clock. See they are inside the café at that hour, and you may return and join Pyke for a meal at The Seven Stars.'

Evidently he was not going to allow Dorothy and me to wander round Chollerford unattended. We walked back to the Town Hall, and he waited for us until Simkins reappeared without the parcels.

'Shall I order what I think suitable for Dorothy at the dressmakers, sir?' I asked.

'Yes. By all means.' With a smile and a wave, he disappeared into the stone building.

'Where be you going, miss?' asked the footman.

'To the dressmakers, first,' I said. 'But while we are in there, you can reserve a table at the café. We shall be quite a long time at the dressmakers,' I added. 'You will have time for a stroll round the town while we are there.'

He gave a wide grin. 'Thank 'ee, miss.'

Weynells, the shop we were bound for, was quite a pretentious establishment. They had a good selection of materials inside, also ribbons and laces, and haberdashery of all kinds. They had a book with various fashions illustrated, and you could choose the style you wanted. On the next floor was the dressmaking part of the shop, where a dressmaker and her two assistants measured and cut out material, and fitted customers. They also sold babies and childrens' clothes, petticoats, stockings and stays, and wools and silks to knit and crochet.

Together, Dorothy and I looked at the materials. Her father had said she could have anything which I thought suitable. I thought a navy blue cloak would be serviceable for everyday wear, and a cream-coloured coat and bonnet for churchgoing, and other occasions. I ordered three dresses in different patterns of printed cotton for her, and various other things, including two broderie anglaise dresses for evenings. Dorothy had helped to choose the styles of the cotton dresses, and she was wildly excited at these purchases.

I then ordered a pale blue costume for myself. There were other things I would have liked to buy, but I did not wish to do all my shopping with

Dorothy there. It would be nice if I could sometimes use the carriage to come into Chollerford by myself, I reflected. Absurd thought — how quickly a luxury could become a necessity.

I gave the name of Tregarth to the assistant, but said that the costume I had ordered for myself was on a separate account. We had timed things quite well; Simkins appeared in the shop just as we finished there.

'We have time to stroll around before we go to the café,' I told Dorothy. I took her hand, and the footman followed closely.

'Can we go and see what they are selling?' enquired Dorothy, looking at the groups of people milling around the market stalls.

'Very well,' I said, for I could see no harm in it. It was a scene of colour and liveliness. There was livestock for sale, rabbits and puppies, chicks and caged birds. There was a gypsy selling lace and ribbons, her face as brown and shrivelled as a withered apple. There was a stall with toffee, and a man standing talking about his wonderful, cure-all bottle of medicine. There were ugly ornaments, drinking glasses, cups and saucers, new laid eggs and cakes and buns. There was even a man promising to extract teeth painlessly, although nobody appeared to be taking him up on this. Dorothy's eyes were wide with wonder, she kept pointing and exclaiming, and I kept telling her not to point.

'Ah, let me tell you something, my lady,' said the gypsy, pushing in front of me. 'You have a lucky face — buy some lace, and I'll tell you.'

I smilingly declined, but Dorothy shook my hand, crying excitedly, 'Buy some lace, Miss Mountjoy! Go on, buy some!'

Thus urged, I said I would have a yard.

'Yes, my lady! There is a fine house for you! There are servants — I speak the truth!' Half laughing, half annoyed that I had been persuaded by Dorothy, I handed a coin to her, in exchange for some lace.

'You have an enemy — be on your guard. But after the harvest your troubles will be over — wait, there is more! There is a gentleman — he is sad — '

'Come on, Dorothy,' I said, moving hurriedly away with my charge. I could feel my cheeks burning. If Dorothy repeated all this to her father, what would he think?

'It is all nonsense,' I said, dismissing the matter. 'But it is very cheap and pretty lace, and I'll whip it on to your doll's dress.'

'Perhaps I had better go first, it's so crowded here, miss,' suggested Simkins tactfully, after the incident of the gypsy. Accordingly he led the way through the throng of farmers, waggoners, thatchers and shepherds, the latter in their long smock-frocks.

'I think we had better go for luncheon now,' I said, when we had looked our fill. Accordingly we walked over the cobblestones up the narrow hilly lanes to Byner Street.

'I've got 'ee a table by the window,' said Simkins. 'I thought Miss Dorothy would like it.' He was a likeable and trustworthy man, and it was strange to me now to think how nervous I had been when he had first answered the door to me.

'Very well. We will be all right now. You may go,' I told him, as we entered the place. I had been there once or twice before. It was not large inside, there being only a few tables, most of which were occupied. I explained to the waitress that a gentleman would shortly be joining us, and she said they were serving soup, roast pork and vegetables. I hoped this would meet with Mr. Tregarth's approval, but as far as I knew there was nowhere else suitable for taking Dorothy. While I was thinking about this, her father appeared at the door.

'We're here, Papa!' cried Dorothy. He

smiled at us both, and gave a quick glance round. I knew then that it was all right. The waitress hurried over to take his order. It was, I knew, quite plain food, but it was also good.

'We've been to the dressmaker,' said Dorothy importantly. 'And I'm going to have all sorts of clothes — a new coat and bonnet, and two white dresses for evenings — and Miss Mountjoy is going to have a new costume.'

'You've certainly been busy,' said her father, with a smile. 'And I'm pleased to say I shan't be needed at court again after luncheon. So we will be able to drive back.'

'And I shall be able to skip,' said Dorothy blissfully. 'Miss Mountjoy bought some lace from a gypsy, Papa, and the gypsy told her she had a lucky face. And she said — '

'She talked absolute nonsense, Dorothy,' I interposed quickly, catching Mr. Tregarth's questioning gaze. 'Dorothy wanted to look at the market stalls, sir, and I could see no harm in it. I hope you have no objections.'

'Simkins was with you, wasn't he?'

'Yes.'

'Then I have no objections. She should see a little of the world outside. This is quite a good luncheon of its kind, Miss Mountjoy. Should you have occasion to travel into Chollerford with Dorothy any time, you may bring her here, if it is necessary to stay in the town for luncheon.'

I was pleased that the shopping expedition had been so enjoyable and successful. Although I still felt a bit ill at ease with Mr. Tregarth, he seemed satisfied with me up to now. Otherwise he would not have permitted me to choose the books so freely, nor Dorothy's clothes, for that matter. As we drove back through the winding, hilly lanes, I wondered why Miss Hepton had not suggested new clothes for the child. But then, perhaps she had, although I felt it was more likely that she was not sufficiently interested in Dorothy's appearance to bother.

I wondered what the child's mother had been like, and what kind of life they had led in Italy.

As soon as we alighted from the carriage, Dorothy dashed ahead to the nursery, where the footman was bound with her parcels, and I thought it best to hurry after her. When I arrived at the nursery, she had already undone the parcel containing her toys. She was wildly batting the shuttlecock all over the place, with Simkins watching her, grinning.

'That's the way, Miss Dorothy! Only you're supposed to keep on hitting it.'

'Look at me! Look at me!' she squealed.

Simkins gave his head a little shake, and disappeared downstairs. He had completed his duties. I unpacked the books, and made Dorothy sit down.

'Now listen to me, Dorothy,' I said. 'You have had a very nice day out, and we've ordered some new clothes for you, and your father has bought you some toys. But we have also bought books and things for your lessons, and tomorrow we are going to have some. When you have worked hard, you may play with the shuttlecock, or whatever you want to. And when we go out for a walk, you can bring your skipping rope. But I won't allow you to play with anything unless you do your lessons first.'

'I'll do them,' said Dorothy instantly. 'I'll work ever so hard. Miss Mountjoy, may I skip now?'

'Very well. Today you may skip. In the schoolroom, though.' She dashed off with the skipping rope, and I could hear her feet thudding all over the place. There was a crash, as a chair was knocked over. She was certainly a handful.

She came back into the nursery a few minutes later. 'Miss Mountjoy, have you got a sweetheart?'

'No, of course not! Your head is stuffed with the nonsense Rosie has told you.'

'But that gypsy said something about

a gentleman — I heard her!'

'Nobody takes any notice of what gypsies say, Dorothy.'

'Don't you want a sweetheart?'

'No. Now you can read this picture book with me.'

At dinner that evening, Miss Hepton was dressed in a lovely mauve-coloured gown. How governessy I felt in my white lace blouse and black skirt. This was the one time when Dorothy really behaved herself; the thought of being deprived of this treat kept her quiet and good. Her father was discussing the events of the day with Miss Hepton.

'We had a very good day out,' he told her. 'Fortunately, I only needed to attend court in the morning. Miss Mountjoy bought books, and ordered new clothes for Dorothy.'

'Splendid,' said Miss Hepton, glancing at me with patronizing dislike.

'Miss Mountjoy knows of quite a good dressmaker in Chollerford,' he said, after the soup was served.

'I've heard there is a dressmaker of

sorts there. Well enough for Dorothy at her age, I've no doubt. Later on she will want most of her clothes made in London, I expect, like me.'

At the close of the meal, Mr. Tregarth told the butler to serve the port in the library. 'You may come and play there with me for half an hour,' he told Dorothy. 'Then Miss Mountjoy will take you up to the nursery again.'

We rose from the table. 'Has Miss Mountjoy seen your apartments here yet?' enquired Mr. Tregarth of Miss Hepton. 'I know it will take her some time to get to know everywhere, but I think she should see your rooms.'

Was there a hint of authority in his voice? I stood without speaking.

'Yes, certainly,' said Miss Hepton. 'I am free this evening, and she can spend the next half hour with me, before duty calls her again.'

With a rather smug smile, she walked ahead of me out of the dining room. As I followed her, I noticed how beautifully her gown was cut, and how perfectly it was moulded over her bustle. Did she have her own maid? These questions and many more, went through my mind as I followed her down the long corridors to the rooms where she and her father had lived for so long, and, presumably, saved Lionel Tregarth from a life of utter loneliness.

5

'This is my sitting room,' said Miss Hepton proudly. She led me into a charming room, full of pretty tables, pictures and bric-a-brac. Wine-coloured curtains and a gold and cream patterned Brussels carpet gave the room an air of richness and comfort. Then I noticed that in spite of the plants in the room, and the flowers placed on little tables, there were photographs of men in military uniform on the walls, and curious mementoes around the place; a carved table with a dagger on it; a set of pipes in a rack.

'When my father was alive, we both used this room,' said Miss Hepton, as if she were reading my thoughts.

'It is very nice,' I said. 'I see from the view outside that it is on the same side of the house as the nursery.'

'Yes. Uncle Lionel only used the

library and the morning room, and Papa thought it best if we used this wing of the house, and kept it in order.'

She showed me her dining room, and again I was impressed by its elegance and good taste. So she had her own dining room; why, then, did she take her meals with Howard Tregarth? She could, if she chose, lead a completely separate life. Still, few men would expect her to do that, particularly as she was accustomed to having the run of the house.

'My bedroom is across here.' I thought how bewildering all these corridors were. She unlocked the door of a room, and ushered me in. It was delightful, with everything as dainty and comfortable as possible. How lovely her dressing-table was, with the silver brushes gleaming upon it.

There was no heavy curtaining on the fourposter bed, only the prettiest of white, frilled muslin. She had a writing desk and a bookcase; a chaise-longue, and an enormous wardrobe, filled, I had no doubt, with fashionable and expensive clothes.

'I have my own maid, Tessa. She does everything for me, but naturally, the housemaids attend to the rooms. I breakfast here every morning.'

I felt that she wanted me to see and realize how very different her position was in this house from my own. We walked back into her sitting room, where, somewhat condescendingly, she invited me to sit down. I did so, and she took the chair opposite.

'Naturally, there is a great deal which Mr. Tregarth doesn't know about the house — and the estate in general. My father attended to all the practical matters for Uncle Lionel. Papa was a very keen horseman, and he used to hunt — I used to go with him. Uncle Lionel had hunted at one time, but he took no interest in it for many years. Papa and I were free to entertain whenever we wished. I have many friends. I am helping Mr. Tregarth to index all the books in the library. There is such a lot to do here. He used to worry about Dorothy, but I told him she was well enough with Rosie to look after her for a few months. I used to bring her in here sometimes, and play the piano for her. As you know, I act as Mr. Tregarth's hostess. He was a bit worried about that at first — fearful for my reputation, naturally, but then, who would be likely to spread malicious gossip? Certainly not the servants, they understand the situation, and certainly not my friends. Mr. Tregarth and I get along very well indeed. Employing you is a good thing, though. He will be less concerned about Dorothy's welfare now she has a governess. Dorothy is a minx, though, and needs firm handling. She is too boisterous for me to stand for very long.'

That was pretty well what I had thought. But how Miss Hepton ran on. She was not gossiping, so much as letting me know just how powerful her position was in that house.

'You won't be sleeping in the night

nursery for much longer,' she said, when it was almost time for me to go. 'The Blue Room will be ready in a day or so.'

'Thank you,' I said. I rose to collect my charge from the library, Rather to my surprise, Miss Hepton rose too.

'I must remind Mr. Tregarth about something,' she explained. 'There is so much to think about.' Together we went to the library. She tapped on the door and opened it without waiting for permission. Mr. Tregarth and his daughter were playing a children's card game together.

'There, I told you time was up,' he said cheerfully. 'Put the cards away now, Dorothy.'

'I forgot to mention something which I noticed while out riding today,' said Miss Hepton brightly, advancing into the room. 'I thought you ought to know about it — '

I took Dorothy back to the nursery. I had a feeling Miss Hepton had gone to the library on some flimsy pretext, just an excuse to see Mr. Tregarth again. After his daughter was in bed, I sat in the nursery, and thought about Miss Hepton's charming apartments. I contrasted her position with mine, and I would not have been human if I had not felt a pang of envy. Then I thought of her in the library with Howard Tregarth. How much did he like her? For she liked him, I knew. Yes, more than liked him. No doubt she had many admirers, but put her in my position, and how different everything would be. Sitting in the nursery of that big house, I suddenly felt terribly alone.

The only person I could confide in at all was Old Mollie, and there were things which she couldn't understand. Despite my neatly braided hair and governessy clothes, I longed to love and be loved in return. But the man would have to be a very special person, not one of the village boys.

Later on I unpinned my long, dark tresses, and prepared for bed. I had no lady's maid to dance attendance on me, as Miss Hepton had; no one to dress my hair and care for my clothes. But things could have been very much worse; at least I had a position, and I had been promised a home of my own when the mill-house was let to somebody else.

★　★　★

'There's a funny smell,' said Dorothy, wrinkling her nose. 'Don't you think so, Miss Mountjoy?'

'It's because the room hasn't been used for such a long time,' I said, looking round with approval. The Blue Room was now ready for me, and I would have been hard to please if I had not liked it. Dorothy was very interested, too, as she had not seen it before, except when it was under all the dust sheets.

The furniture was of rosewood, with a lovely dressing-table and wardrobe. There was a writing desk, too, a comfortable chair, and a splendid fourposter bed. But the most striking and unusual feature of the room was on the wall; a huge tapestry depicting The Last Supper, with Jesus and the disciples at the table. We both went to it with one accord, and examined it. It was beautifully worked, and at the bottom was embroidered the name Jane Tregarth, and the year 1804. Dorothy touched it, almost with awe.

'Yes, Dorothy,' I said. 'You've just started to learn embroidery. Just think how long that must have taken to do! Years and years.'

'Who did it?'

'Try to read the name.'

'Why, it's Tregarth! The same as mine!'

'Jane Tregarth,' I said. 'And she sat and embroidered it a long time ago.'

'Who was she?'

'Perhaps your papa could tell you that. It's certainly beautiful.'

'And is she dead now?'

'I should think so.'

'Like Mama.' It was the first time she

had mentioned her mother, and I felt it was a good thing.

'It's a nice room, isn't it?' I looked through the window.

'Yes, but it's haunted. Rosie says so. It's haunted by a lady who walks around crying. All the servants say it's haunted.'

'Well, I'm not afraid of the ghost,' I said. 'If I hear it crying, I shall ask it why it's crying.'

'I shall have to sleep alone tonight,' said Dorothy.

'I've told you, you have your nightlight, and if you wake in the night you can always come to me. But you won't wake, you'll sleep until morning.'

She put her thin little arms around me, and I hugged and kissed her. It wasn't just discipline that Dorothy needed, it was love and tenderness as well.

That evening, as soon as dinner was over, she mentioned the tapestry to her father.

'I believe Jane Tregarth would be a

great-aunt of mine,' he said. 'So she would be your great-great aunt, Dorothy.' Then he turned to me. 'I trust you find the room satisfactory?'

'Very much so, thank you. I shall be moving in tonight.'

'Papa, is it true that the room is haunted?'

'Of course not, you goose. There is no such thing as a haunted room.'

'I know what she means,' said Miss Hepton, rising to leave the table, with a sour little smile on her face. 'I expect she's heard some of the servants' gossip. There is supposed to be a lady who walks about, wringing her hands and weeping — '

'Really? What extraordinary imaginations people have,' was Mr. Tregarth's comment, as he prepared to take his daughter to the library for her usual half hour with him. 'It's as well Miss Mountjoy is not of a nervous disposition. At the same time, this ridiculous gossip about a ghost could be upsetting to a child. I don't know how these rumours get about.'

Miss Hepton made no reply, but left the table, with the fixed little smile still on her face. Later on that evening, long after my charge was in bed, I sat in my room, crocheting a shawl for her. When it grew dusk, I lit the lamp. There were great, dark shadows on the walls; I could see the faces of the disciples on the tapestry. I marvelled again at the size of it, and the long hours which must have been entailed in the working of it. It was true that there was a slightly musty smell in the room, but as everywhere had been cleaned thoroughly by the maids, it was just the smell of an unused room, and should soon go now it was occupied.

I sat by the fireplace reading, when I grew tired of crocheting. There was a sudden sound, which caused me to start. Before that the room had been silent, save for the ticking of the clock. What was it? I felt an icy chill creep through me. The story which Rosie had told Dorothy, and which Miss Hepton knew about, came back to me. It was the faint, low, sound of someone crying!

It couldn't be, though. It was ridiculous ... I didn't believe in anything like that.

I listened, straining my ears. All was silent again. If you listened, you could always hear sounds in old houses. The mill-house used to creak dreadfully in a strong wind.

Then I heard it again. It was quite unmistakably the sound of sobbing. I stood up, my heart pounding.

'Who is there?' I cried. There was no reply. I opened the bedroom door, and looked at the passage outside. There was no one there. I opened the door of the night nursery, but Dorothy was sleeping soundly. Feeling afraid and uneasy, I went back into my room again.

All was quiet. I waited, listening, but there was still no sound. I proceeded to undress, still straining my ears. After some time, I went to bed, but lay wakeful, wondering if it had been imagination on my part. At last, overcome by tiredness, I fell asleep.

The following morning I thought about it as I made my toilet. I had never believed in the existence of ghosts, although I knew that a lot of old houses were reputed to be haunted. I had always thought that these stories were made up by the servants, to frighten new scullery maids. I had not cared for my first night in the Blue Room at all, but I could hardly say so. Imagine what Howard Tregarth would think, if I told him that room *was* haunted, after all! Besides, what of Dorothy? I had laughed her fears to scorn. I examined the room closely in the morning light.

My fears of the previous night seemed ridiculous. Drawn by the beautiful tapestry, I stood looking at it again. It was not properly framed as it should have been, just stretched and nailed onto the wall. There were two outside walls to my room, and now I noticed that the one with The Last Supper on had several patches on the faded wallpaper, quite close to the edge of the tapestry. The room needed redecorating — probably replastering, too. If the tapestry was left there to take its chance, the damp would ruin it in time.

As for the sobbing, the sensible thing to do, I decided, was to pretend it had never happened. I was my usual, cheerful self when I went in to Dorothy. Rosie brought our breakfast up to the nursery, and afterwards I gave Dorothy a reading lesson. As I expected, her first question was to ask me if I had seen or heard anything of the ghost, to which I replied that I certainly had not.

6

'He's been no trouble, my lovely. But he's been round to the mill-house every day, and he do sit there waiting for you.'

It had taken me a long time to calm Barnaby; his excitement and joy at seeing me again knew no bounds. I had sat and talked to Mollie half the morning, and she had listened eagerly. It was good to sit in her rather untidy kitchen again, and share a meal with her. I told her all about my life at Abinger Hall, and about Dorothy and her father, the young Squire. I also told her about Miss Hepton.

'Ah, a young lady, be she? And she be sharing the house at the present time?' Mollie nodded her head knowingly. 'And he be a young widower, too. She'll be setting her cap at him, you see if she don't.'

She spooned some broth out into two

bowls. In spite of the fact that Barnaby had missed me, he looked in good health, and I knew he was being well fed. 'Yes,' repeated Mollie. 'There'll be a wedding at Abinger Hall. You see.'

'Well, my position should be safe,' I said. 'Wedding or no wedding.' Mollie's broth was as good as ever. She had not known I was coming, but I knew she seldom stirred from her cottage, and if she went to shop in the village, it was always in the morning. I had been driven here in the dogcart by Charles, one of the grooms. He had relatives in Bramwell, and he had arranged to visit them, and call for me later. I had left the mill-house key with Mollie, so that she could see all was well there, but I intended to go and see for myself. Accordingly, some time later, I strolled along to the mill-house, with Barnaby racing ahead of me. As soon as I opened the door, he rushed through it, and ran all over the house, barking joyfully.

Poor old dog, he thought I had come

back, and that he was going to live in the mill-house again. I felt a sudden sadness as I stood in the flagstoned kitchen, with its peeling paintwork, and broken window. It looked such a forlorn place, after the great spacious rooms at Abinger Hall. Mollie had been looking after my hens, and having the eggs, but I had promised Dorothy I would take her back a few eggs, as she seemed to think there would be something special about them.

Her lessons were progressing satisfactorily. It was true that she found it difficult to sit still and concentrate for long, but as she was such an inquisitive child, I felt that once she could read she would want books very much. I dusted and swept the mill-house, and as I did so, I thought of her request that I should bring her with me. I knew that she wanted to see the mill-house, and Barnaby, and Old Mollie. I doubted if her father would care for the idea, though. Then I fell to thinking about the first night I had slept in the Blue

Room, and how certain I had been that I had heard the sound of crying. Since then, though, all had been quiet, and I half believed it *had* been my imagination.

To my surprise, there was a knock at the door. Barnaby barked madly, and I went to open it, trying to quieten him down as I did so. A man of about thirty stood there, a bold looking fellow in a suit of navy blue broadcloth.

'Good day, miss. I was just having a look around, but I saw you through the window. They said in the village that I wouldn't find you here.' His eyes went slowly over me. 'I'm from Chollerford, and I deal in grain. I've milled before now, but not in these parts. They say this mill is going to start again, and that the Squire be looking for a miller. Is it true?'

I was so completely taken by surprise that for a moment I didn't reply. He stood in the doorway, in the warm sunshine, his dark eyes staring into mine, bold and admiring.

'Well, yes, it is true,' I said slowly, thinking that I could certainly not ask him in. Barnaby stood growling.

'That being so, I'm interested,' were the stranger's next words. 'Are you living here?'

'If you are interested, then you should see the Squire, or the man who deals with his affairs,' I said coldly, seeing no reason why I should tell him all my private affairs.

'They say in the village that you don't live here,' he went on. 'They say you work for the Squire — governess to his daughter.'

'Do they? Why do you ask me anything, then? You can find out all you want to know in the village.'

'I found out your name ... Miss Mountjoy,' he continued unabashed. 'Mine is Abel Wilks. I would be obliged if you could show me around the place.' He did not say what he meant by 'place', but I was certainly not going to ask him in the house.

'I'll show you the mill,' I said, after

some hesitation. I took the key and walked to the mill with him, Barnaby dancing round at our feet.

'They say it's not been used for a great many years,' said the stranger. 'Is that so?'

'Yes. It was last worked by my father, before I was born. I had a look in not long ago, but that was the first time it had been opened for years. You'll have to see if you can turn the key. It's very stiff.'

He put the key in the door, and turned it slowly, in much the same way as George Hansbury had done. Once again the dark, odorous interior was revealed. Abel Wilks looked around, and made to ascend the stairs.

'I believe those steps are unsafe,' I said. 'I don't know much about it, of course.' He was already up the stairs, and looking around. I stood in the doorway with Barnaby, who sat down, no longer very interested. After a while, Wilks came down again.

'It needs cleaning up, and a few

repairs doing,' he said. 'I suppose the millwheel and everything will need attention. But once that is done, it should be all right.' I stood and waited while he locked up again.

'So you never remember the mill being worked?' he asked.

'No, never.'

'Well, they say the old Squire never bothered about anything. And you've lived in the mill-house a long time?'

'As a matter of fact,' I said, 'I've lived in it all my life.'

'But not now?'

I was annoyed by these many questions, but I thought that under the circumstances I had better tell him the plain truth.

'It is for my use until after the harvest,' I said. 'I am a governess at Abinger Hall now, so I live there. But I am here today to see that everything is in good order. I shall be having a cottage made ready for me, so that I still have a home in the village. I don't really like to give up the mill-house, but apparently it goes with the mill.'

'If I came here as miller . . . ' He left the sentence unfinished, his bold eyes appraising me again.

'I'm afraid I must go now. Good day,' I said, and went back into the house, leaving him standing there. The impudent way he was looking at me filled me with frustrated annoyance. I went back to Mollie's, with the dog at my heel, wondering if Abel Wilks would become the miller. I told Mollie all about him. As I talked to her, I glanced round the room. Was her suggestion that I should share her cottage the best idea after all? I had known her all my life; if Mr. Tregarth was willing to have a cottage repaired for me, why not have all Mollie's repairs done?

'You're far away, my love,' she remarked, during a pause in the conversation, while I sat thinking about this.

'I've been considering your suggestion for me to share the cottage with you. It might be the best idea, after all.'

Her face brightened. 'I told 'ee to come here! Now you see the sense of it.'

'Yes,' I admitted.

'That man looking at the place will want to move into the mill-house as soon as young Squire be willing, if he gets the position of miller. You're better here with me, than trying to keep all the young men away. Jennie would have thought so, too.'

I felt sudden relief, and at the same time a desire to broach the subject to Howard Tregarth as soon as possible. Charles, the young groom, called for me, and drove me back. I could think of nothing else but the plan to have Mollie's cottage repaired and improved. I received a joyous welcome from Dorothy. She was delighted with the eggs from my hens, and wanted to hear all about Old Mollie.

After dinner that evening, I asked Mr. Tregarth if I might have a few words with him in connection with the mill-house.

'Yes. After Dorothy has gone to bed, I

will be pleased to see you in the library.'

'Thank you, sir,' I said. Later, I went down to the library for Dorothy, and later still I retraced my footsteps, and, feeling somewhat nervous, I knocked on the library door. I was told to enter, and advanced into the room.

'Ah, Miss Mountjoy. My daughter is in bed, I trust?'

'She is, sir.' I sat down on the proffered chair.

'Would you care for a glass of port?' I thought I should accept his offer, and he poured out a glass for himself, and one for me.

'Now, Miss Mountjoy . . . ' He settled back in the chair facing me, and waited for me to speak.

'Well, sir,' I began, after a preliminary sip of wine, 'I have spent most of the day back at the mill-house.' He inclined his head.

'While I was there, I thought matters over, concerning the cottage which you said you would have repaired for me. Mollie Treen, my grandmother's old friend, is willing for me to share her cottage; to regard it as my home when I am not on duty here. It does need quite a number of repairs doing to it, though, and I thought if she could have those done first, then I could see about moving in with her.'

'You prefer this to having one of the cottages in the village made ready for you?'

'I've thought about it, sir, and I do.'

'Then I think you're very sensible,' he said. 'It will be no more trouble, and will require no more labour than doing any other place up. And probably you won't feel so uprooted.'

'Thank you,' I said. 'While I was there today, a man called at the mill-house, and asked me to show him the mill, which I did. He said he had heard that you intended to put a miller in there, and that he was interested.'

'You mean this man was a complete stranger to you?'

'Yes, sir. I have never seen him before.'

'You should have sent him about his business, then, Miss Mountjoy. What goes on in connection with the mill now is not your concern. I am putting an advertisement in the Chollerford Weekly Journal, anyway, so if this man is interested, he will be applying in the right quarter.' He paused a moment, and then continued, 'In any case, it is far better that you should share a cottage. It is a very strange idea for a girl to live alone, as you have been doing in the mill-house.'

'Strange, perhaps, sir, but it is the way circumstances have compelled me to live.' Emboldened by the wine, I continued: 'In much the same way as Miss Hepton, really.'

He glanced at me sharply. 'I see little resemblance,' he said. 'Miss Hepton is far from alone here. But that is by the way. I think your idea of sharing a cottage is a very good one.'

I finished my glass of port.

'Before you go, Miss Mountjoy, we may as well discuss riding lessons for

Dorothy. I understand you do not ride?'

'No, sir.'

'I would like Dorothy to start having lessons, and I think she might find it easier if you were both to start having lessons at the same time. Would you be agreeable to this?'

'Yes, of course. Only — ' I broke off. He raised his eyebrows.

'I have no riding habit,' I said, in some embarrassment.

'I scarcely expected you to have. When you and Dorothy go back to the dressmaker for a fitting, order a riding habit for her, and one for yourself, too. If you like, have them both in the same colour. I shall supply the habit for you, naturally. What is wrong?'

My acute embarrassment must have shown on my face.

'Regard this riding habit as something necessary to your position as governess,' he said. 'Naturally, I do not expect you to go to the expense of supplying it yourself.'

'I would prefer to buy my own riding

habit,' I said quietly.

A look of annoyance passed over his face. 'I can't really see why,' he said. I could hardly explain to him that I had a very independent streak in me, and that although I naturally expected to be paid for my services as his daughter's governess, I had no intention of being beholden to him in any way. He had offered to have a cottage repaired for me, so the fact that it was Mollie's cottage made no difference. I would not ask him for favours, nor would I allow him to buy me a riding habit.

'We seem to have discussed such matters as were necessary. I think we can conclude this interview, Miss Mountjoy,' he said.

I stood up to go. 'Thank you. I'm very pleased that the repairs to Mollie's cottage will be done.' He gave me a somewhat curt nod of dismissal as I left the room.

Mr. Tregarth was not an easy man to understand. Certainly he had his own ideas about the way Abinger Hall should be run. He did not like to be overruled; he was clearly displeased by the way I had insisted on buying my own riding habit. And he saw little resemblance between my circumstances and Miss Hepton's . . .

Outwardly, of course, there was little resemblance. Except that she had been left living in property which belonged to him, in actual fact. But unlike me, she had not received notice to quit after the harvest. *She* was living in the same house as the young Squire, completely unchaperoned, except in the sense that there were plenty of servants about, as well as Dorothy and myself.

I thought of Old Mollie's prophecy that there would be a wedding at Abinger Hall. There would if Miss Hepton had her way. I was convinced that she hoped to get Howard Tregarth as a husband. She wanted Abinger Hall. I could tell by the way she talked about it, and by the way she walked about in it, that her dearest wish was to be mistress of it.

After repairing a doll's dress in the nursery, I went into my own room. The window was open, but that faintly damp, mouldy smell lingered. It seemed to me to be particularly strong round the tapestry. I sat in the chair by the fireplace, reading, as I usually did in the evenings. Occasionally my attention wandered, and I would put down my book, and think with pleasurable anticipation of the riding lessons I was going to have.

Later on, when I was on the point of going to bed, I heard a sound. I stood up and listened, my heart pounding. Yes, there was no mistaking it. It was the faint sound of sobbing. I knew this time that it was not imagination. Someone was crying, but where? It seemed to be in the room, yet not in the room. As before, I went into the night nursery, but Dorothy was sound asleep. For a moment I stood there, feeling quite unnerved. I did not feel in the least inclined to go back to that room, and spend the night there. In spite of my brave words to Dorothy about there being no such things as ghosts and hauntings, I was by no means sure now.

What could I do about it, though? I tried to imagine telling Mr. Tregarth about the sobbing; his eyebrows would certainly be raised in disbelief. Miss Hepton would give her icily contemptuous little smile — no, I would have to keep silent. In any case, if it got to Dorothy's ears that I was afraid of the alleged ghost, and had heard it crying, she would become panic stricken.

I sat quietly in the night nursery for a long time. Then I went reluctantly back to the Blue Room. As on the previous occasion, all was silent. I undressed, and got hastily into bed. There was no sound, and I finally went to sleep.

★   ★   ★

It was morning, and the first thing I heard was the beating of heavy rain on the window. I went to look out. The sky was dark grey, and the distant hills shrouded in mist. It was early yet; later on it might clear up. I hoped so, as Dorothy pined and fretted if she could not go out. Then I fell to thinking of the night before, and the crying. It was so easy to be brave in the morning. My glance was drawn to the tapestry and I noticed fresh patches of damp round it. The wind was obviously driving the rain straight at it. I went up to it, and examined it more closely. The edges of the tapestry were getting damp. I suddenly realised that this was what was causing the smell. The tapestry was probably mildewed at the back; it would be ruined in time. Should I mention it to Mr. Tregarth? I decided that I would. Accordingly, later that morning I tapped on the library door. Mr. Tregarth bade me enter, but I was somewhat discountenanced to find Miss Hepton there too. They appeared to be extremely busy, sorting through a large pile of books.

'I'm sorry to trouble you, sir,' I said. 'But the damp appears to be coming into my room quite badly, and I fear it will completely ruin the tapestry which is up. Also, it makes the room smell very musty.'

'In that case, Miss Mountjoy, we will have it removed,' he said briskly. 'I don't want the tapestry ruined, it must be very valuable. Nor do I want you to have to suffer an unpleasant smell. I'll instruct Simkins to take it down, and it can be dried out, before it is damaged. And I shall have the wall attended to if the damp is coming in like that. It shouldn't be.'

I thanked him, and left the room, feeling glad that something was to be done about it. That afternoon, while I was in the schoolroom with Dorothy, Simkins appeared with a stepladder, a hammer, and some pincers, and said that if it was convenient for me, he would like to take the tapestry down then.

'Let me watch! I want to see it being taken down,' cried Dorothy immediately.

'Very well,' I said, because I wanted to watch, too. The three of us went into the Blue Room.

'It shouldn't take long. I've just got to get they nails out, miss.'

It took longer than expected, though. After a few minutes, Dorothy became bored, and said she would come back later. We went back into the school-room. I realized that it was going to take longer than Simkins had thought; it was a big tapestry, and well nailed down. After some time we went back, and found him loosening the last couple of nails.

'There be no wallpaper — no plaster even on this wall, miss,' he said. 'It just be the stones. That's why the damp is coming through.'

'How very strange,' I said, looking at the expanse of stones revealed. I could see clearly the mark where the tapestry had been; there was a neat, two inch frame of plaster where it had been nailed on. Within that frame the stones of the wall were uncovered.

'Why is it like that, Miss Mountjoy?' asked Dorothy. She looked up at the stones, wrinkling her nose at the musty smell.

'Some of the mortar came away when I took the tapestry down, Miss Dorothy. Don't 'ee touch they stones, or you will bring more down, and a fine mess it will be in Miss Mountjoy's room. We'll have to get one of the maids to sweep the floor as it is.' Simkins carried the great, impressive tapestry away to the kitchen, to be dried. I went back to the school-room with Dorothy, thinking how uninviting my room looked now, and how I would be more than pleased to vacate it while the necessary replastering and decorating was being done.

That evening Dorothy and I had our dinner served in the nursery, as Mr. Tregarth and Miss Hepton were dining out; whether together or singly, I was not sure. It had been a long, wet, tedious day, and I was not sorry when I finally kissed Dorothy goodnight. The rest of the evening stretched ahead, not very enticingly. I did not wish to sit in my own room, with the gaping stones at one wall, and the dank smell. Most of all, though, it was the muffled, terrifying sound of that weeping which kept me out.

Eventually I would have to go in there to sleep, but I had no doubt that when I told Mr. Tregarth about the bare stones, and the fact that the smell was worse than ever, he would want me to move out of it immediately.

Later on in the evening, drawn by mingled fascination and fear, I went out of the nursery, and into the Blue Room. The maid had swept up the bits of rubble and mortar which had fallen on the floor while Simkins had been removing the tapestry. Then I noticed that he had left the hammer behind. I went up to the musty smelling expanse of stones, and examined them carefully. A good deal of mortar had come away from one of them.

Moved by a curiosity which I could not have explained, I brought a chair over, and stood on it. Suppose I knocked away the remaining mortar from that stone? I picked up the hammer, and began tapping with the sharp side of the head.

Bit by bit the mortar came away, and a wide chink was revealed. I caught my breath sharply, as suddenly I could see what appeared to be a fragment of rotting material. I could not stop now, and went on, tap, tap, tap, until finally the stone was loose enough for me to remove. Slowly and carefully I took it out. The rotting material was revealed, but there was something else sticking out of the fabric. It was a strange, oriental looking bracelet. Fascinated, I stared at it. It appeared to be made of very tarnished silver; it was in the shape of a snake, with dull, red stones for eyes. I put the sharp side of the hammer head under the fabric, and gently lifted it. A bone was revealed, a bone with the bracelet round it.

I knew then that I had seen enough. Feeling violently sick, I replaced the stone, and fled back to the nursery. I was shaking from head to foot. *There was something in the wall!* The tapestry had been used to hide it. I could never, never, sleep in that room again. I wanted to rush and tell Mr. Tregarth about my gruesome discovery, but I knew that he was out. I would have to wait until morning, but meanwhile, I would make up the bed in the night nursery. When I had calmed down a little, and summoned up sufficient courage, I entered the Blue Room again, and removed the bed linen. I shuddered as my eyes were again drawn to the place where the Last Supper had hung. What grisly secret had that beautiful tapestry concealed? Whatever it was, it would certainly have to be kept from Dorothy. Later on, even in the shabby security of the night nursery, I lay shivering, shocked by what I had seen. In the morning I would have to tell her I had slept there because my own room was too damp.

* * *

Sunshine brought in the next day, and in that bright and pleasant light, with the sound of the birdsong, I could almost have deluded myself that the discovery of the night before had been imagination.

With Dorothy I behaved as though all was normal, but as soon as she settled down with her painting book, I sought out Mr. Tregarth. It was too early for him to be out of the house, I thought. Most likely he would be in the library. In fact, he was alone in the breakfast room, obviously just finishing his meal. Evidently he was breakfasting late, after having been out late the night before. I felt embarrassed at seeking him out like this, but under the circumstances, I wanted to tell him about the Blue Room as soon as possible.

'I'm sorry to trouble you at this hour, sir,' I said, 'but I discovered something in my room last night which I think you should know about as soon as possible.

I would have told you last night, if you had not been out.'

'Indeed,' said Mr. Tregarth, setting down his coffee cup. 'Might I ask what this discovery is, if it is so urgent?' He indicated a chair.

'Simkins removed the tapestry yesterday,' I said, sitting down. 'He found there was no wallpaper underneath it — no plaster, even. Just the stones, and the damp, musty smell seemed worse than ever. Some of the mortar had come away, and last night I investigated the stones, and took one out, and found — ' I broke off, at the remembered horror of it.

'Yes, Miss Mountjoy. What did you find?'

'There was some rotting material, and — and a bracelet — and I moved the material — and — I could see something else — '

'Yes?' he said gently.

'I could see a bone. The bracelet was round it. I went back into the nursery for a while. Then I took the sheets off my bed, and made the bed up in the night nursery. I can't sleep in that room again.'

'You will not be expected to. I shall have the matter investigated straight away. Naturally, I don't want Dorothy to know anything about this. It may not be as bad as you think.'

'I hope it isn't,' I said. 'But whether it is or not, rest assured I will keep Dorothy away from the room, and keep silent about what I have seen.' I went back to the schoolroom then, feeling considerably better for having told him. As it was a fine day, I was out a good deal with Dorothy, and kept her away from the Blue Room.

Before nightfall, though, I knew what the tapestry had been concealing. The skeleton of a woman was removed from the wall. She had been put there still wearing a wedding ring, and with the bracelet I had stared at, on her wrist.

7

'Here you are, Miss Dorothy,' said Pyke. 'Here's old Starry, for you. He couldn't be more gentle — and a nice horse for Miss Mountjoy. You bain't be afraid, be you?'

'Of course not,' said Dorothy stoutly. We stood in the stableyard with Mr. Tregarth and Pyke. The young groom, Charles, was there too.

'Well, now, let's get 'ee both into the saddle,' said Pyke, and he and Charles helped us both up.

'Now I'll lead yours, Miss Dorothy, and Charles will lead Miss Mountjoy's.'

Very slowly, we began to move along. 'Go with the horse,' said Pyke. 'Is that stirrup all right, Miss Dorothy?'

'Yes,' said Dorothy. 'It bumps you up and down a bit, doesn't it, Miss Mountjoy?'

'Yes, it does,' I agreed. 'But your

pony, Starry, looks very nice. We must make proper friends of them, Dorothy.' Her father had told me in private that she had witnessed a carriage accident when she was about four years old. The horse had been rolling about on the ground, and she had screamed with terror at the sight of the great mane-tossed head, and open mouth. He thought, and he was probably right, that this had caused her nervousness of horses. He was very eager for her to overcome this, so that she could enjoy riding.

The fact that I was learning at the same time was a good idea. I had seen with envy the effortless ease with which Miss Hepton galloped her grey hunter about. She looked very well on horseback; something which she was clearly aware of. We progressed out of the stableyard and onto the grass. It was a fine, sunny day, and as we went slowly along, I began to feel more confident.

Mr. Tregarth had told me to put behind me the gruesome secret of the

Blue Room. It had been established that the remains had been there for many years, and although the police had made enquiries, so far they had not been able to establish the identity of the woman. Certainly no one at Abinger Hall knew anything about the matter, although naturally there had been a good deal of gossiping among the servants. Acting under Mr. Tregarth's instructions, I told Rosie that if she breathed one word to Dorothy, she would be dismissed instantly. He told me that the bracelet which I had seen, and the wedding ring, were now Crown property, and were being kept at Chollerford Police Station for the time being. The Blue Room was locked up once more, and I had a pleasant room a bit further away from the night nursery.

And on that warm, bright morning, I felt only too ready to put the horrifying memory to one side, and concentrate on my riding lesson.

'I'm getting used to it now, Miss Mountjoy,' called Dorothy. 'It's just that

I feel a bit high up.'

'Yes, I feel high up, too,' I said. 'But riding on an elephant must be a lot higher.'

While we were having our lesson, Miss Hepton appeared on her big, grey horse. She smiled in a superior manner.

'A first lesson, I suppose,' she said, and then urged her splendid horse forward at a gallop, showing without words what an excellent horsewoman she was.

I knew that she was both contemptuous because I couldn't ride, and jealous because I was having lessons. We spent another hour being taken slowly round by Charles and Pyke, then Mr. Tregarth came strolling along.

'Look, Papa!' cried Dorothy. 'I can ride!' She sat proudly in the saddle, and I saw pride on her father's face, too.

'Splendid,' he said.

'And Miss Mountjoy can ride,' she added, indicating me on my mount.

'Miss Mountjoy is splendid, too,' he said gravely. Then he caught my eye, and there was a look in his which I could not fathom. 'You both look splendid on horseback,' he said lightly, and left us quite abruptly.

The Boldwoods from Tyzanger Grange were dining at Abinger Hall that evening, so I knew that Dorothy and I would not be going down to dinner. I was just as well pleased, as I found Miss Hepton's manner towards me very difficult to bear at times. Dorothy had been pleased to find I was sleeping in the night nursery again, and disappointed when I had another room made ready for me. I went and sat in it that evening, after Dorothy had gone to bed.

In spite of Mr. Tregarth's good advice, as usual when I was alone, the memory of what had been found in the Blue Room came back to me. To think that I had slept there, and not known the grisly secret behind the tapestry! I thought, too, of the sobbing which I had twice heard there, and about which I had not told a soul. *Was* the room haunted? And was the ghost at rest, now? I knew that the remains had been decently interred, even though the identity of the woman remained a mystery.

I was in a very nice room now. True, the gold wallpaper was faded, as were the matching curtains at the fourposter bed and window, but it boasted a rocking chair, and a fine mahogany bedroom suite. It was certainly an improvement on the Blue Room, in that it was pleasant and unremarkable, with no ghosts reputed to haunt it. Nevertheless, I could not put to one side the memory of that dank smell, the sound of sobbing, and the dreadful discovery which I had made. How long had those remains been walled up behind that tapestry? And what other strange secrets did Abinger Hall conceal?

I made a determined effort to put these morbid thoughts to one side. I thought instead how concerned Howard Tregarth had been that I had been sleeping in a room which contained a skeleton, and how kind he had been towards me.

To my surprise, after my riding lesson with Dorothy the following morning, he sent for me. He was in the library, and as I tapped on the door, I wondered why he wished to see me.

There were two other men in the room, one of whom I knew acted as steward for Mr. Tregarth, a man called Samuel Druridge, and the other one was the bold looking fellow who had come to the mill-house. He grinned at me straight away.

'Ah, Miss Mountjoy,' said Mr. Tregarth, briskly, offering me a chair, 'you mentioned someone enquiring about the mill some time ago, did you not?'

'Yes, sir.'

'The position of miller has now been filled. Normally Druridge would have attended to all this, but it's the question of the mill-house being empty now which I want to discuss with you. You have already met Abel Wilks. We propose to get the mill in good working order as soon as possible, so that after the harvest it will be going at full tilt. It's the question of the mill-house.'

'Yes?' I prompted.

Abel Wilks spoke up. 'It's like this, miss. I'd like to move into the mill-house as soon as possible. I shall be going into Chollerford on market days as usual. As you be not living in the house — and Mr. Tregarth do say you're going to share the cottage nearby with an old lady — can I move into the mill-house now?'

I sat hesitating.

'Mr. Tregarth says the rent be paid up to the end of June. I will make that right with you, miss, and — '

'But what about the furniture?' I asked.

'I'll take good care of it, and when the cottage is repaired, you can take what furniture you want, and I'll buy the rest.'

'Do I understand you are not married, Wilks?' interposed Mr. Tregarth.

'Not yet, sir.'

Mr. Tregarth turned to me. 'What do you think of the idea, Miss Mountjoy?'

On the face of it, it seemed a very good one. Mr. Tregarth must have decided the man was suitable, and there was no real reason why I should not fall in with these plans.

'It seems to be an agreeable arrangement,' I said, turning to Abel Wilks. 'Mrs. Treen in the cottage has the key. However, I think I had better go and explain everything to her. Otherwise she would not know whether to give the key up or not.'

'I have my waggon with me. I could take you now,' offered Abel Wilks, his eyes openly admiring.

'I'm afraid it's not convenient today,' said Howard Tregarth decisively. 'Miss Mountjoy is teaching my daughter in the schoolroom. I will make arrangements to have her driven there tomorrow.'

Abel Wilks looked a trifle disappointed, but I was glad to abide by Mr.

Tregarth's decision. 'I think, then, the matter is settled,' he added. 'You had better see what Dorothy is doing in your absence.'

I left the library, thinking about this fresh turn of events.

'What did Papa want you for?' was Dorothy's eager demand, and I explained about the miller. She expressed a wish to see the mill-house. She was eager to see where I used to live, and also, she wanted to see Old Mollie. I told her that we would arrange it sometime, if her father was willing.

At dinner that evening, Miss Hepton eyed me with her customary dislike. 'Did you notice the way they have changed the gardens at Tyzanger Grange?' she enquired of Mr. Tregarth. She seemed as if she wanted me to know they had been visiting there together. From what she had said, she had been there frequently with her uncle. I knew that Mr. and Mrs. Boldwood were middle-aged, but they had a daughter, Kate, who was unmarried, and about the same age as Miss Hepton. They also had a son a few years older.

When the meal was over, I saw Dorothy looking at her father with expectant dark eyes. Miss Hepton glanced across at her, and I saw in that look a singular lack of tenderness. It crossed my mind that if, as Mollie had suggested, there would be a wedding at Abinger Hall, Miss Hepton would have precious little time for Dorothy when she became her step-daughter.

'Very well, Puss. Half an hour in the library,' said Mr. Tregarth, smiling at his daughter.

I went up to the nursery, and looked through the window. The day had spoilt itself by becoming showery, and there were dark clouds over the distant hills, otherwise I might have strolled on the terrace for a while.

Dorothy always insisted that I should go down and bring her up from the library every night. I was sure Miss Hepton had made an excuse to go with me that time she had shown me her rooms, but she could hardly do that every time. When I tapped at the library door, Dorothy ran to open it, and said that her father wished to speak to me.

'It was only to say that the dogcart will be at your disposal tomorrow, if you wish to see to your business affairs in the village,' he said.

'Papa, may I go, too?'

'No. Miss Mountjoy has to see about some matters in connection with her house.'

'But may I go with her *sometime*, Papa?'

He looked across at me. 'That is up to Miss Mountjoy.'

'If your Papa is willing, then you may come with me another time,' I said. Dorothy clapped her hands with glee, kissed her father goodnight, and danced ahead of me up to the nursery. The blue sash on her white dress came undone, and so did the ribbon in her hair. I followed her, smiling. She had got her own way, and that was very dear to her.

8

'They be going to mend the thatching on the roof, and do the window sashes, and do all sorts, my love,' said Mollie, a note of satisfaction in her voice. 'Two men, there be, and they say they won't be long with it, either. And then they're going to do up the mill-house, and the mill.' She really looked pleased about it.

After a good deal of preliminary barking, Barnaby had settled down beside my chair, and was gazing up at me. I had only been in the cottage a few minutes, during which time Mollie had done most of the talking.

'I'm going to have a look at the mill-house,' I said. 'There is a new tenant coming in, Mollie.'

'What, so soon?'

'The man I told you about, who came and asked to be shown the mill has got the position of miller, and wants to move into the mill-house as soon as pssible.'

'And will you let him?'

'Under the circumstances, yes. He says he will give me what payment we agree upon for the use of the furniture, and when I move in here with you, he will buy any furniture I don't require.'

'Well!' exclaimed Mollie. 'Aren't things working out well for you after all? It was a blessed day for you when you went to see the young Squire.'

'It was indeed,' I agreed. Mollie rose, and accompanied me to the mill-house. Barnaby barked and gambolled around in the sunshine. I looked at the untended garden, and felt a little sad.

We entered the mill-house, where all seemed as usual.

'You'd best bring your bed linen and anything else you want over to my place,' said Mollie.

I went upstairs, and into the room where I had slept, with Barnaby at the foot of the bed. How poor and miserable it looked, after my room at

Abinger Hall. I took out one or two articles which were in the dressing-table, and then went into my grandmother's room. The big, sagging feather bed looked as it always had, with the bright patchwork quilt on, which my grandmother had made when she had been a young bride. There was linen in the worn chest-of-drawers, and as I emptied it, the perfume of lavender filled the room. She had always dried it, and put it in the drawers. Being in her room and smelling the lavender which she had put away so carefully, brought her back to me vividly. I thought of her lying on that bed, and the last, strange words which she had spoken: 'Unconsecrated ground . . . like a dog . . . '

'They'll soon be starting to clear the millwheel, and do repairs there shortly,' said Mollie, as we carried the things over to her cottage, making more than one journey.

'Yes. And when Abel Wilks comes for the key of the mill-house, you can give him it, Mollie.'

'I'll do that, my love. But what about the hens? I feed them every day.'

'I'll ask him if he wants them,' I said. 'Otherwise it would mean you would have to go to the mill-house, or else have them here.'

For some time we talked things over. Mollie sat, nodding her head. I had not mentioned to her the remains which had been found in my room. I knew that Mr. Tregarth did not care to have the matter gossiped about, and I felt bound by loyalty to discuss it with no one.

When I left Mollie, and went back to Abinger Hall in the dogcart, I realised how much she had missed me, and how she was looking forward to my next visit. Being dependent on the dogcart was beginning to irk me, though. I was becoming a good deal more confident in the saddle now, and I could not help thinking how convenient it would be for me if I could ride over and see Mollie. Sometimes I might want to spend the night at her cottage, and to be able to borrow a horse would be very useful.

Naturally I would have to approach Mr. Tregarth about this matter, and the time was not yet ripe to do this.

As we turned in at the gates of Abinger Hall, Dorothy stood in the drive, waiting for the dogcart. It was duly stopped so that she could get in beside me.

'You've been a long time,' she said accusingly. 'Tell me what you've been doing.'

'You tell me what you've been doing.'

'I went out with my skipping rope, and then I went into the kitchen, and Cookie gave me some cake, and I looked at the kittens, and they're big now. I played with them, and Cookie and Rosie asked me where you were, and they talked about — er — all sorts. Miss Mountjoy, what is a will?'

'A will? Why do you ask?'

'I sat under the kitchen table, and nursed one of the kittens, and they were talking about the old Squire.'

'Dorothy, I wish you wouldn't listen

to all this kitchen gossip. Your papa would not like it.'

'He doesn't know I was there. But what is a will?'

'It's something which a person leaves, saying what they want to be done with all their things after they die.'

'Oh. They said it was a funny business at the Hall these days. They said it would be different if he had left a will, but nobody could ever make him. They said his heart was broken — what did they mean, Miss Mountjoy?'

'Please, Dorothy, you must not repeat this gossip. And they had no right to be talking like that when you were there.'

'What is repeat? And they didn't know I was there, they thought I had gone out, because I sat as quiet as a mouse under the table. And then I sprang out laughing, when I couldn't sit still any longer. They jumped, and said: 'Oh, Miss Dorothy, don't 'ee go saying nothing about what you've heard'.'

I repressed an inclination to laugh at Dorothy's excellent mimicry of the West

Country dialect. 'You had no business to be there listening,' I said severely. 'And you mustn't talk about what you've heard — that is what repeating it means.'

'But I can repeat it to you, can't I?'

I hesitated, feeling it was wrong to encourage Dorothy's tendency to listen to gossip, but at the same time, a child needed someone to confide in.

'Very well. You can tell me what you heard, but not now. Wait until we are alone, getting ready for dinner.'

Although clearly bursting with information, she sat and listened while I told her about Mollie and Barnaby, and the hens. No sooner had we entered the nursery, though, than she began to chatter again.

'Miss Mountjoy, I can repeat things now, can't I? Cookie was boasting about how long she had been here — longer than anyone except Pyke. But she said when she first came here she was a scullery maid, and worked her way up to being cook. She said she used

168

to help Mrs. Brown, who was very close-mouthed about everything. What did she mean?'

'I expect she meant Mrs. Brown didn't gossip.'

'She said Mrs. Brown passed on suddenly, and she had been here for nineteen years — Cookie has, I mean. She said she thought the old Squire might have left her something, but he didn't make a will. She said he didn't care what happened to Abinger Hall any more after his son dis — er — disgracing the family, and dying abroad. She said the old Squire cut him off with a shilling. What did she mean? Papa gives me a shilling sometimes.'

'It's too difficult to explain,' I said. I was brushing and plaiting her hair while she talked.

'Anyway, she said she was a French dancer. Who did Cookie mean?'

'I don't know, Dorothy.'

'Then she said Mrs. Brown used to say, ask no questions, and you'll get no lies told.'

'Very wise, too.'

'Then Cookie said it was one in the eye for *her* anyway, him not leaving a will. She said some people hoped they would be settled here for good, with a part share in the house. But Cookie said she and all the servants knew there had been no will, and nobody had got a ha'penny out of the old Squire. She said so much for the colonel's influence, not to mention *hers*. And then she said Tregarths always do what they want to do, anyway, but the old Squire didn't want to do anything, and the estate had to go to . . . ' I tied her plaits with ribbon. 'To go to some word I can't remember.'

'Probate?' I suggested, interested in spite of myself.

'Yes. I think that was the word. And she said the young Squire was the er — nearest relative. She means Papa, doesn't she?'

'Yes, she means your papa.'

'But Cookie said, you see, she won't give up without a struggle. And Rosie laughed, and said good luck to her. But Cookie said the present — er — something, couldn't go on for ever.'

'Situation?'

'I think that was it. And then I came out from under the table, and Cookie went all red.'

'You shouldn't have been there at all. And now you've told me everything, you should feel better. And if you can remember your lessons like you remember gossip, you should do very well.'

'When we lived in Italy, the servants used to speak in Italian. They sometimes forgot I spoke it too, and so I used to hear a lot. They used to talk . . . about Mama.' I saw a shadow cross Dorothy's small, pale face. I knew now that she had an excellent memory for the spoken word; what fragments of Italian gossip were tucked away in her mind?

'Tell me about your mama,' I said.

'She used to play with me sometimes. But some days I never saw her. Sometimes she used to lie down all day.

And I used to drive out with Carla, Mama's maid, and Uncle Kiki used to wait for the carriage, and give me sweets and money, and talk to Carla, and give her a note for Mama.'

'Uncle Kiki?'

'He was a secret between me and Mama. She used to give me sweets and money too, and make me promise not to tell anyone about Uncle Kiki.'

'Not even . . . your papa?' I asked. Having listened to Dorothy's account of the cook's conversation, I seemed to have released some inner spring. Her face was animated; for the first time she seemed eager to talk about her mother, and her life in Italy.

'No, I hadn't to tell Papa. Carla knew, of course.'

'Go on,' I said.

'Sometimes Mama went out in the carriage by herself, and I had to pretend to Papa afterwards that I had been with her, too. She used to give me kisses, as well as sweets.'

I realised then that Dorothy had been

desperate for her mother's love. The picture she painted of their life in Italy sounded a very strange one. Who was the mysterious Uncle Kiki? The atmosphere Dorothy had lived in seemed to have been one of corruption and deceit. Untrustworthy governesses; a maid who conspired with the child to deceive her father, and a mother who bribed her to do the same thing. The surprising thing was that the child had emerged seemingly untouched by these experiences.

'Was your mama pretty?' I asked.

'Yes. She had a face and hair like Violet.'

'Violet? Oh, you mean your doll.' I had a sudden vision of a blonde, blue-eyed woman, with a pink-and-white complexion. Dorothy did not resemble her in looks, then.

'Mama was often ill. She would lie in her bedroom, and be cross with everyone. I liked it when she was well enough to drive out alone, and when she came back she would be smiling and happy. Then she stopped getting up at all, and the doctor came every day.'

She stopped speaking.

'Go on,' I said, gently.

'One day Papa took me into her room, and she was lying with her eyes shut, not speaking. Papa told me to kiss her, and she opened her eyes, and he took me out of the room again. I stayed in the nursery with Carla, and I saw a carriage drive up to the door. I saw Uncle Kiki get out, and go into the house. I said to Carla: 'Look, there's Uncle Kiki', and she began to cry. She said that Papa had sent for him, so that he could see Mama. After a long time, Uncle Kiki came out of the house, and he had a handkerchief held over his face. Papa came to the nursery door, and he whispered something to Carla, and she began to cry again. Then he picked me up and kissed me, and told me that Mama would not be in any more pain, and that I still had him, but that Mama wouldn't come back again. And Carla lit candles and prayed with her rosary, and all the servants were crying.'

Her childish voice stopped, but the curiously vivid picture which she had painted, of her life in Italy, and of her mother's death, had impressed me with its simple clarity. I seemed to feel and remember with her the weeping servants and the lighted candles the day her mother died. And why had her father sent for this mysterious Uncle Kiki? It sounded a suspicious relationship to me, but perhaps the child had got some of her facts wrong.

'And then,' I said, 'what happened then?'

'After the funeral, Papa said we would stay in Italy for a little while, but we would come back to live in England. And then one day he said we would have to return straight away, because Uncle Lionel had died, and we would be living in Abinger Hall. He said it would be a new life for both of us. I cried when we left Italy. So did Carla, but Papa wouldn't bring her with us'

'Well,' I said. 'I think that's enough for now, Dorothy. I'm going to get ready too.'

'I can repeat things to you, can't I?'

'Yes. You can repeat things to me.' Far better and safer to say that, I thought. As I made my toilet, I realised that Dorothy was capable of keeping silent about things close to her heart, even though she could be something of a chatterbox in other ways. She had wept on leaving Italy, and had wanted the Italian maid to come with them, but her father had not brought the girl. If he had liked and trusted her, he may well have done so. Perhaps he had been glad to leave Italy and all its memories behind him. I pulled myself up sharply as I finished doing my hair. Why was I so interested?

Later, at the dining table, Mr. Tregarth asked if I had made suitable arrangements concerning the mill and mill-house.

'Really, this mill business seems to be of extraordinary importance,' remarked

Miss Hepton, a trifle impatiently, over her soup. 'As nobody has bothered about the place for twenty years or so, I hardly see the urgency now.'

'Possibly not,' said Mr. Tregarth drily. Miss Hepton changed her tack altogether, and remarked that she had heard there should be a bumper harvest that year.

'I hope so. I intend to have a harvest supper here in any case.'

'A harvest supper?' she repeated, looking very surprised. I saw Dorothy's eyes wide with excitement.

'Yes. At one time the harvest supper was a regular thing here, but that was a long time ago. The older people remember it, though, and I see no reason why this custom should not be revived. I have no wish to isolate myself from the villagers to the extent that my uncle did. I have been very busy since I came to live here, but I hope to take an interest in some of the things they do. Do you think they would like that, Miss Mountjoy?'

'I'm sure they would,' I said. 'In fact, I think a number of the villagers have felt somewhat neglected for a long time now.'

That evening I went to my room for a shawl, and strolled on the terrace until it was time to bring Dorothy from the library. As I walked up and down, I thought about what the child had told me before dinner. So the old Squire had not left a will, and Howard Tregarth had inherited because he was next-of-kin, and for no other reason. And if there was no will, Miss Hepton was not remaining here because of any written wishes expressed by Lionel Tregarth. It was very plain who the 'she' was that the servants had been talking about; plainer still what they were hinting at. Celia Hepton was playing out a rather desperate game, knowing, as the cook had said, that the present situation at Abinger Hall could not last for ever.

Much later that night, long after Dorothy was in bed, I sat in my rocking chair and read. Occasionally my attention would wander from the page, and I would think of her childish confidences, and of the strange picture of their life in Italy, as she had drawn it. Then I would think of the servants' gossip which she had overheard, and wonder about the old Squire's son, and what became of the French dancing girl he was reputed to have married. And then I would think, as I thought every night, of the dreadful discovery in the Blue Room. Had that poor woman been walled up alive? And if she had, who had done it? And why? Who was she?

Little had I known in all the years I had lived in the mill-house, what a strange family the Tregarths were. The rumours that they were unlucky had a certain amount of foundation. There was one thing I was thankful about, anyway. The sound of sobbing late at night had not followed me to my present room. I did not believe in ghosts, but I knew that the crying which I had heard had not been imagination.

★   ★   ★

Dorothy and I were both making good progress with our riding lessons. I asked Pyke how long he thought it would be before I could go to the village on horseback. He raised his shaggy eyebrows.

'Well, miss, it seems to me, not so long now. You have quite a good seat.' It was true; by now I was able to feel quite at home in the saddle, even when the horse was trotting. As I was talking to Pyke, Miss Hepton appeared.

'Lessons as usual?' she enquired. Her riding habit was so well cut, and so obviously expensive that I immediately felt shabby beside her. She walked between our mounts, patting them both, and talking to them. Then, just as she moved away, my horse gave a loud neigh, and sprang forward, lashing out its heels. I screamed; it bucked again, and the next moment I was flung out of the saddle, and onto the cobblestones of the yard. Everything went black. When I came round there were faces bending over me, and I could hear the sound of Dorothy crying loudly.

'Are you all right, miss?' came the anxious voice of Will Pyke. 'I don't know what came over Pete. He's never been like that before. Miss Hepton's gone to fetch help.'

I lay there, feeling sick and dazed.

'Miss Mountjoy — oh, where is Papa? I'm going to tell Papa,' came Dorothy's stricken voice. Someone had brought a chair from the stables, and Charles and Will Pyke helped me onto it. My gaze focussed on Dorothy's white and frightened face. I still felt unable to speak. Rosie came hurrying along, accompanied by Miss Hepton.

'Oh, I see things are not too bad,' said the latter, coolly.

'A drop of brandy — that's what she needs, miss,' said Pyke.

'I've brought some.' That was Rosie.

'Cook gave me it.' I was handed a glass, and coughed as the burning liquid went down my throat. 'How do you feel, miss. Where have you hurt yourself?' went on the maid.

'Don't fuss, so, Rosie,' said Miss Hepton sharply. 'And stop that awful row, Dorothy. It's no use people having ideas about riding if they can't take a tumble from a horse occasionally.'

'I'm all right, Dorothy,' I managed to say, although I was trembling with shock. I tried to smile at her reassuringly.

'Thank the Lord you fell clear,' said Pyke. 'You might have been dragged in the stirrup. Ah, here's the master.'

'Papa! Papa!' Dorothy dashed away, and returned, clinging to her father's arm. 'It's Miss Mountjoy — her horse jumped and kicked, and she fell off!'

'It's all right, Howard. Just a bit of a spill.' So spoke Miss Hepton.

Mr. Tregarth did not appear reassured. Indeed, his face was pale and anxious as he eyed me.

'I shall be well enough in a little while,' I managed to say.

'Where is the horse now?' he asked Pyke.

'He's bolted, sir. Old Pete, the gentlest mount we've got, apart from the pony Miss Dorothy rides. I've never seen him behave like that before.'

'Go for the doctor, Pyke, straight away. How do you feel, now, Miss Mountjoy?'

'I feel much better. I've not broken any bones, I'm sure of that.'

'I prefer the doctor's word on that,' said Howard Tregarth firmly. 'I will assist you into the house, with the aid of Miss Hepton. No, on second thoughts, I'll carry you in myself.'

As he spoke, he bent and picked me up in his arms. Despite the recent shock which I had sustained, I felt extremely embarrassed being borne along in that manner, in front of the servants and Miss Hepton. The latter walked beside us, a look of spiteful resentment on her face. I knew that she would have liked to tear me out of his arms. Dorothy hurried on ahead, her habit tucked up over her arm, shouting at the top of her voice that I would need plenty of cushions when her papa took me into the house.

As he walked along with me in his arms, sudden, strange sensations stirred in me, despite the fact that I was so shaken. The close physical contact of my body pressed against his disturbed me; filled me with an aching longing which in its way seemed as painful as the fall. My first embarrassment left me, and the only feeling I had was of the security of having his arms around me, and the wish to stay close to him.

He carried me into the drawing room, and placed me gently on the chaise-longue. The concern on his face seemed to be too much for Miss Hepton.

'Well,' she said. 'As no harm has been done, although a great fuss made, I shall have my ride. I doubt if any horse could unseat me. Are you having your lesson as usual, Dorothy?'

'No,' said Dorothy immediately. 'I'm never going on a horse again.'

'You mustn't say that, Dorothy,' I said. 'Just because I had a fall.'

'Miss Mountjoy is quite right,' said her father, looking at me with open admiration in his eyes. 'You go back with Aunt Celia, and have your lesson as usual.'

Miss Hepton gave me a glance of baffled fury. Evidently she had hoped that being thrown like that would frighten me off any more riding lessons, and frighten Dorothy at the same time. The child stood, hesitating between a natural fear, and a wish to please her father and me.

'Just a short lesson,' I said coaxingly. 'Just a walk round, to prove that you are not afraid.'

'Very well,' said Dorothy slowly. 'Just a short one.' She left the room with Miss Hepton.

'I can't understand what made such a gentle horse behave like that,' said Mr.

Tregarth, walking over to the window. 'I am terribly sorry this has happened, just when you and Dorothy were both doing so well.'

'Dorothy is all right,' I said quietly. 'She will have a short lesson, and that is the main thing.'

'Yes, thanks to you. You are very brave, Miss Mountjoy.' He turned from the window, and looked at me. Again the strange feelings went through me as I met his gaze. Sensations powerful and tender, heady and frightening, all at once. What was happening to me? It might have been the shock of the fall, but suddenly I longed to feel his arms around me again. More than that, I wanted to feel that firm mouth pressed against mine ... but what was I thinking? These thoughts were foolish — more than that, ridiculous. The ache down my side where I had fallen was becoming more severe.

'I'll probably be stiff tomorrow,' I said.

'If the doctor thinks it necessary, you

must stay in bed. A fall like that is a shock, even if there are no bones broken.' He sat with me, talking quietly until the doctor came. After greeting him, he discreetly left us alone.

'Well, well! So you've had a nasty fall from a horse, eh?' Dr. Fossett was a jolly looking, middle-aged man, with a red face, and a rather grizzled grey beard.

His hands were gentle as he examined me.

'You've been fortunate,' was his verdict. 'It could have been much worse. You'll probably have a few nasty bruises and you're likely to feel a bit shaken up for a day or two, but otherwise, no harm done.'

'Thank you,' I said. Mr. Tregarth was relieved to hear this, but after the doctor left, he told me I must rest for the remainder of the day. 'If you rest in the nursery, Dorothy can play quietly,' he said. 'Ah, here she comes.'

'I've had my lesson!' she cried, rushing into the room.

'Take Miss Mountjoy to the nursery,' said her father. 'You must look after her for the rest of the day, Dorothy.' She seemed rather pleased with this idea. We went up to the nursery, and I sat in the big leather armchair. Dorothy nursed her best doll, and chattered away, telling me she had not been afraid to mount Starry after all. Rosie brought in our luncheon, and asked me how I was. The fact that everyone seemed so concerned about me was rather nice. I was feeling much better now. The sick feeling had left me, and I was able to eat normally. Afterwards I rested in the chair again, and Dorothy looked at picture books. Then she said she was going out for a while.

'Don't go too far away in the grounds alone, then,' I said.

'I won't. I'll just play about the house.' She put on the shawl I had crocheted for her, and skipped out of the room. Left alone, I tried to analyse my feelings towards her father. This was not easy. Something which had been lying dormant had sprung to life that morning. Strange and tumultuous feelings were stirring inside me; feelings which must, perforce, be kept secret from everybody. For what happiness could I ever hope to receive from caring for someone who only saw me as an employee?

Howard Tregarth was the Squire; I was but the miller's daughter. I sat in the armchair, thinking these thoughts.

Before long, Dorothy returned, carrying a handful of pansies. 'Look, Miss Mountjoy, I picked you these myself from the flower beds.'

'That is very kind of you, Dorothy, but Sykes, the gardener, would not be very pleased.'

She laughed. 'I know. He won't find out, though.' She arranged the flowers in the little glass jar she used for her paint water. 'I've been round to the stables again,' she went on. 'And Pete is back in his stall, and he's as good as gold again, Pyke says.'

'I'm pleased to hear that.'

'I found something while I was in the stableyard. I don't know what it is.' She handed me a hatpin. For a long time I looked at it in the palm of my hand. Of course it would not be noticed in the cobbled yard. It was a long, fine pin, with a black head. Somehow Dorothy's bright eyes had caught sight of it, as they caught sight of so many things.

Miss Hepton had one or two fashionable, tipped forward hats. Looking at the hatpin, I knew that she had deliberately jabbed Pete with it, and moved quickly out of the way. She was skilled in dealing with horses. It was an act of such spite that it took my breath away.

'What is it?' asked Dorothy. Her dark eyes were fixed enquiringly upon me, and it seemed to me she too had her secret suspicions concerning that pin. I could not be sure, of course, but in some ways she was less innocent, more devious than most little girls who, unlike her, had been brought up in England. Certainly I must reassure her.

'It's just a pin, dear. Someone must have dropped it.' It would never do to let her know what I thought it had been used for. Besides, I could not prove anything. I could not help thinking how angry Howard Tregarth would be if he knew about it. I might have been badly injured. One thing was certain, I would never allow Celia Hepton anywhere near me again when I was on horseback. I told Dorothy I felt well enough to give her a reading lesson.

That evening I dressed carefully, and went down to dinner.

'Why, Miss Mountjoy, you should have had your dinner served upstairs,' exclaimed Mr. Tregarth, on seeing me.

'I've been resting all day. I feel quite well, now, except for some soreness,' I said. 'And I understand Pete is back to normal now — as good as gold, Pyke says. I don't think he will cause any more trouble.'

'Umm, we can't be too sure about that, although it's funny for a normally gentle horse to turn nasty, unless it's provoked.'

'Perhaps he was provoked,' I said innocently, as I started my soup. I looked at Miss Hepton as I spoke. Was it my imagination, or did she look momentarily startled?

'I don't see how.' Mr. Tregarth looked thoughtful.

'Well, bees and wasps are around now, I suppose. He might have been stung. I know how it feels — just like a pin being thrust into you.' I glanced in Miss Hepton's direction again, and was rewarded to see she had coloured up. I had no doubt at all but that she had maddened the animal with sudden pain. It would have been easy for me to have said more, but I thought it was better to leave it at that.

'Some people would not make so light of it,' was Mr. Tregarth's comment. I knew that would not please Miss Hepton, and I was glad of it. Fortunately her spiteful and irresponsible act had done me no harm, but it had done her no good. I caught Howard Tregarth's eye, and lowered mine. He must never know what feelings had been released in me that day. The remainder of the evening passed as usual. Dorothy went to the library with her father.

While she was there, I sat at the window of my room, and looked out across the parkland. The long, curving drive stretched out in the light of a summer evening, with the shadows from the trees lengthening on the grass. I could see the lodge gates in the distance, and within those gates I had an enemy.

9

'Miss Mountjoy, come and have a look round the boathouse,' said Dorothy.

I was sitting on the banks of the river, watching it slide noiselessly along. Kingcups and buttercups were massed around me, and the air was full of summer scents. It was haymaking time; a warm and sunny day in June, and Dorothy and I were spending the afternoon out of doors.

'Very well,' I said. 'I'll look round it, but that's all.' She was, as usual, dashing here and there, and I had a shrewd idea why she wanted me to look at the boathouse. It was just a small one, containing one quite serviceable looking rowing boat, a pair of oars, a hammer, and sundry other tools. She ran inside, and perching herself on the side of the boat, grinned at me.

'Let's go on the river, Miss Mountjoy. Please!'

'No, Dorothy. I can't row, and it could be very dangerous.'

She pulled a face, and stood up. I wondered when the boat had last been used, and by whom. There was a little landing stage beside the boathouse.

'Pick some flowers,' I said. 'You may go and play. But don't lose sight of me, and don't go too close to the edge of the bank.'

'I never do,' she said sulkily. She walked away with a slightly crestfallen air. I knew that it wouldn't last long, she soon got over her ill humour when she saw I was not to be coaxed into anything. I watched the small figure in the printed cotton dress, intending to walk after her before very long. Just as I was on the point of doing so, she turned and started to run towards me. She stumbled and fell in the long grass, but jumped up and hurried on, covered in yellow pollen.

As soon as she was within earshot,

she began to shout excitedly.

'Miss Mountjoy, there's a door under the water down here! What is it for? Come and look, and tell me what it is.'

I rose, smiling, and walked towards her. She was forever making new discoveries of some sort, and they were all so exciting and important to Dorothy. She was over excited anyway today, as it was her ninth birthday, and she was being excused lessons.

'Very well, show me where it is,' I said, holding her hand. She hurried eagerly along the bank, to where there was a distinct dip in it, and a few yards further along, she indicated what she had found. Below the level of the water there was a metal door with a bolt held by staples. It appeared well rusted; if Dorothy's sharp eyes had not seen it, I doubted if I would have noticed it myself.

'What is it?' she asked eagerly.

'Well ... ' I began hesitantly. 'I suppose it's ... well, I don't know. I just don't know.'

'Will there be anything behind that door?'

'Certainly not! What could there be — ' I broke off, as the memory of what had been behind the tapestry came back to me.

'This part of the river is funny, isn't it?' went on Dorothy.

'Well, yes, it is in a way. The bank is funny here,' I agreed. 'But tomorrow you can see what the Sedge is like further along. You can come with me in the dogcart, and see Old Mollie, and the mill-house, and everything.'

'You've asked Papa about it, then?'

'Yes. He doesn't mind your going.'

'He's pleased because I can read,' said Dorothy astutely, picking a bunch of buttercups. 'And because I can ride.'

Since I had been thrown off Pete's back, Miss Hepton had not come near me during our riding lessons, and I'd had no more trouble. Indeed, I was now so proficient that I intended to ask if I could go into Bramwell on horseback in future. Dorothy was riding quite well, too. I had been afraid that she might have lost her nerve after Pete had bucked that morning, but it had not affected her. I think this was largely due to the fact that I had made as little fuss as possible at the time.

Her success with reading and riding had filled her with a sense of achievement, and her father was delighted with her progress. Despite all this, though, I was neither happy nor content. The thing which was constantly on my mind, the thing which kept me awake at night, and filled my waking hours with a kind of sweet unhappiness was the certain knowledge that I was in love with Howard Tregarth. I could not explain why or how this had come about, but I knew it had. Just to be under the same roof as him was a source of joy in itself. There were times when I experienced other feelings, too; feelings which were almost unbearable.

These were the occasions when I saw him engaged in conversation with Miss Hepton, or when he had guests, and

Dorothy and I dined together in the nursery. On this particular evening, though, we were going to have a celebration dinner in honour of Dorothy's birthday. I had made myself a simple gown for the occasion. It was only of blue muslin, but I had taken great pains with it, and I thought it suited me very well. I had also made a dress for Dorothy, as a birthday gift. It was pink, and lace-trimmed, and I knew she would be delighted with it.

'Well, Dorothy,' I said, glancing at my watch, 'you've shown me the door thing under the water, and I think it must be time for tea, now.' I knew that Mr. Tregarth had spent the day at Choller-ford, attending court. Dorothy began to get very excited after tea, and it was a hard task to keep her amused until it was time to get dressed for dinner.

'Here is your birthday gift from me,' I said, holding up her new dress.

'Oh, Miss Mountjoy; Thank you, thank you — it's beautiful! Even better than my broderie anglaise one.' With particular care, I helped Dorothy with her toilet that evening. I brushed her dark hair out in little waves. The colour of the dress became her well; she turned away from the mirror with a sudden, imperious little movement, and for the first time I saw a hint of the beauty and grace which would one day be hers.

'Now I'm going to get ready,' I said. I too took particular care to look my best — was it not a special occasion? When I was ready, Dorothy looked at me admiringly.

'You look beautiful, Miss Mountjoy.'

'So do you, Dorothy.' She hugged me excitedly. We went down to the drawing room together. Mr. Tregarth and Miss Hepton were already there. Miss Hepton was wearing a gown which I had not seen before. It was a deeper shade of blue than mine, and I could tell at a glance that it was made of silk.

'Do you like my dress, Papa?' was Dorothy's immediate cry. 'It's Miss Mountjoy's birthday present to me.

Isn't it lovely?' She twirled around to be admired. 'Miss Mountjoy made her own dress, too,' she added.

'Your dress is lovely, Dorothy,' said her father. His eyes met mine, and there was admiration in them; I could feel my pulses quicken.

'Miss Mountjoy is very talented. Her dress is lovely, too. In fact,' he added gallantly, 'I am singularly fortunate in dining with three ladies who all look so charming.'

Miss Hepton gave a tight little smile. 'My word, you have been busy, Miss Mountjoy,' she said. 'The dresses have less of a home-made appearance than one might expect. Indeed, you could probably set up as a dressmaker as well as a governess.'

I ignored Miss Hepton's remark, so, too, did Howard Tregarth. We had not been in the drawing room long before dinner was served, and we entered the dining room, Dorothy clinging to her father's arm, while I, willy nilly, was obliged to follow with Miss Hepton.

Although Dorothy already had my gift, it was understood that she would not be receiving Miss Hepton's, nor her father's until after dinner. This evening, she could chatter all she wanted to at the table. She had been allowed to choose the menu. She had chosen asparagus soup, salmon with cucumber, fried sweetbreads, lamb cutlets, and green peas. This was followed by vol-au-vent of strawberries, and then, with a great flourish, an iced birthday cake with nine candles was brought to the table. Dorothy's face was flushed with excitement.

'Light the candles, light them, Papa!' Her father did so, and I told her to blow them out and make a wish.

'What a quaint custom,' murmured Miss Hepton. Dorothy pursed up her lips, and blew with all her might. Two candles were left alight.

'Never mind, have another try,' said her father. This time she was successful, and, putting his large hand over her little one, the butler helped her cut the first slice. He then left the room, as the parlourmaid had already brought the coffee. We all had a small slice of cake, and Dorothy radiated happiness and satisfaction. Her usually pale face looked pink and pretty; I saw her father glance at her with pride, and then look at me. The atmosphere at that table seemed charged with unspoken emotions.

I was torn between wild happiness, and the sobering knowledge that I was being ridiculous. As for Miss Hepton, I could guess at her feelings, which were anything but charitable towards me. I knew that she had an elderly aunt who lived alone in London. The natural thing for a young lady in Miss Hepton's position would be to take herself and her belongings there, and share a house with her late father's sister. I had an idea she would only do that as a last resort. Before then, she would do everything in her power to gain Howard Tregarth as a husband.

'Miss Mountjoy, you've not been

listening to what I've been saying,' cried Dorothy accusingly.

'I'm sorry, Dorothy,' I laughed. 'Just for a moment, my attention wandered.'

'Here's a cup of coffee. This will wake you up,' said Miss Hepton tartly, handing me it. I knew that her unpleasant manner would not do her any good in Howard Tregarth's eyes. He smiled at me, and I thought again how boyish and carefree he could look on occasions. We left the table shortly afterwards, and retired to the drawing room. Miss Hepton handed Dorothy a parcel in some pretty wrapping paper. Inside was a box of beautifully inlaid wood. Miss Hepton turned the key, and raised the lid. It was a musical box; the tiny figure of a ballerina twirled and pirouetted to the tune of a Strauss waltz. It was obviously a very expensive gift indeed, and Dorothy was delighted with it.

'Well, now you can all come and see *my* gift,' remarked Mr. Tregarth, when Dorothy had played it several times.

'It's not in the house.'

'Not in the house? Where is it Papa?'

'Follow me.' We all went out into the warm, June evening. Dorothy walked with her father, and, perforce, Miss Hepton and I followed behind. I could smell the faint perfume which clung to her, and hear the soft swish of her silken gown. She did not speak to me as we walked along. I soon realised that Mr. Tregarth was going round the back of the house, and towards the stables. Dorothy soon realised this, too.

'Papa, tell me, is it in the stables? Is it in the stables?' He only laughed at her eager questioning. By now I had a good idea what it would be. Pyke appeared, grinning broadly.

'Arrh, Miss Dorothy, we've got something for 'ee.' He led us to a stall with a beautiful chestnut and white pony in it.

'Oh!' gasped Dorothy. 'Oh, Papa, is he mine? Really all mine?'

'He is, Dorothy. A pony of your very own!' The pride and tenderness on his face, looking at Dorothy's delighted one, seemed too much for Miss Hepton. I saw the scarcely masked impatience on hers.

'Look, Aunt Celia! Look, Miss Mountjoy! What is he called, Papa?'

'He's called Toby,' said her father.

'He's beautiful! Oh, thank you, Papa! I can ride on him tomorrow, can't I, Pyke?'

'If Mr. Tregarth says so, Miss Dorothy.'

'Certainly you can ride on him tomorrow.'

'Oh — I forgot. I'm going to Bramwell in the dogcart tomorrow, with Miss Mountjoy. I'll ride on him the next day, then. I'll ride with you, Papa. And Miss Mountjoy can come, too.'

'Perhaps we can all ride together,' he suggested tactfully.

'I'm afraid I couldn't ride gladly with beginners,' said Miss Hepton quickly. It was as well she said so, because I had no intention of riding with her under any circumstances.

After a good deal of further petting of the new pony, we strolled round the house, and walked on the terrace. Miss Hepton was not very talkative, but she did ask me if the men had started to repair the mill.

'I'm not sure what's happening just now,' I said. 'I'm going there tomorrow to see how Mollie's repairs are going on. I hope they don't upset her too much, turning the place upside down. But I don't suppose they will. She doesn't seem to mind, as long as the repairs get done.'

'Papa used to row me right down the river as far as the mill-house, when I was a child,' remarked Miss Hepton. 'I remember that funny little cottage by the bank.'

After a while we went back into the house, and Dorothy was allowed to stay up late. In the drawing room, I played some of her favourite tunes, and we played guessing games, and various other favourites. At last her father said it was her bedtime.

'Don't shut yourself away after Dorothy is in bed,' he said to me. 'This is still a special occasion. Come back to the drawing room and take a glass of wine with Miss Hepton and me.'

As I kissed Dorothy goodnight, she asked me if I wanted to know what she had wished for.

'No, you mustn't tell anyone,' I said. 'Not until it comes true.'

'Oh!' She was disappointed. 'Can't I even say what it was about?'

'It's better not to. Just keep it a special secret.' I went into my own room, and noticed that I was flushed, and my eyes were shining as much as Dorothy's. I dabbed a little eau-de-cologne on my temples. My heart was pounding with excitement. The prospect of spending the rest of the evening in the company of Howard Tregarth was an unexpected pleasure. Naturally, Miss Hepton would be there also, but that could not be helped. Mr. Tregarth gave me a welcoming smile when I returned to the drawing room; Miss Hepton eyed me with her customary glance. He poured wine for the three of us.

'What would you ladies care to do, this evening? I could have had guests, I suppose, but I hardly thought it was fitting for a child's birthday.'

'We might play whist,' suggested Miss Hepton. 'As there are only three of us, we will have to play solo.'

'As you wish. Do you play, Miss Mountjoy?'

'I do. Not with any degree of skill, though.'

'It is no matter.'

'My father was very fond of card games,' said Miss Hepton. She shuffled the pack with a practised hand, and dealt. We played for the rest of the evening, game after game, in which I consistently lost. Mr. Tregarth won sometimes, but not as often as Miss Hepton. There was no doubt that she was a skilled card player, and my constant losing was a source of some pleasure to her. Mr. Tregarth was kind and encouraging towards me; he gave a rueful little smile, and said he thought we were both outclassed by Miss Hepton.

'But they do say, unlucky at cards, lucky at love, Miss Mountjoy,' he said cheerfully. That remark did not please the expert card player.

The long, light, June evening had darkened at last. Miss Hepton declared herself hungry, and sandwiches and coffee were served in the drawing room.

'You and Dorothy are having a trip to Bramwell, tomorrow, aren't you?' remarked Mr. Tregarth to me.

'Yes. Dorothy has been wanting to come for some time. I hope it is a fine day. I'm sure she will enjoy it.'

'They used to say an old witch lived in the cottage by the mill-house when I was a child,' said Miss Hepton.

'Naturally they would,' was Mr. Tregarth's comment, before I could reply. 'In this part of the country, any old villager living in a cottage by herself is bound to be a witch. Likewise, all large old houses like Abinger Hall are haunted. What would people do without their ghosts and witches?'

I thought it better to say nothing. I knew that Mr. Tregarth thought ghosts and witches were nonsense, but I had heard sobbing in the Blue Room, and the tapestry had concealed a grisly secret . . .

The conversation then turned to more general matters; the hour grew late, and I felt it was time to retire, although Miss Hepton appeared in no hurry to do so.

Mr. Tregarth, however, remarked that he was tired, after sitting on the Bench at Chollerford, arranging to bring the pony home for Dorothy, and various other things. We walked into the hall, and took a candle each to light us to bed.

'Good night, ladies. Thank you both for giving Dorothy such a happy evening,' he said simply. He then made his way towards the library. I wondered if he wanted to get a book to read himself to sleep. Miss Hepton and I went to our respective rooms. I did not bother to light the lamp, but undressed in the flickering flame of candle light. Slowly and carefully I removed my muslin gown. A few minutes later I stood in my cotton nightdress, my long, dark hair falling about my shoulders. Outside, I heard the cry of a screech owl, and then it was silent again. I tumbled into bed, and thought about Howard Tregarth, and my love for him. Just to be in the same room as him filled me with joy. It had not crossed my mind, though, that he could possibly care for me, until very recently.

But now, was it possible that he did? I felt sure that he did not care for Miss Hepton. She would never get him for a husband. And yet he would not — could not — marry me, a mere governess, whose father had been a miller. Perhaps after all I had been mistaken; perhaps he was only being kind and polite to me, because I was a nobody. And so I lay in bed, as I so often did now, with my thoughts chasing round and round, until at last I fell asleep.

* * *

'Ah! So this be the little maid from the Hall.' Mollie gazed down at Dorothy, who appeared a trifle shy in her presence. It was another cloudless summer day, and we had arrived at the cottage to find great activity going on. A man was putting in a new window frame, and a thatcher was attending to the roof.

'It will be done by the end of the week, they say,' said Mollie, with evident satisfaction. 'I never thought it would be so soon.'

'Make sure you get everything done now they are here,' I said. 'I might persuade them to tidy up the garden, too.'

'Ah — well, they might, my love. Abel Wilks has been in the mill-house a few days now,' was Mollie's next remark. I reached out and patted Barnaby, who had barked himself hoarse for several minutes after our arrival. Mollie was preparing a meal for us, in her usual haphazard manner, and I decided to see if Abel Wilks was around the place at all. Dorothy had got over her first shyness, and agreed to stay at the cottage while I went to the mill-house. I told her she could see it before we went back. How strange it seemed to be once more walking along the familiar path on the river bank; to be passing the well again. I walked up to the door, and banged the brass knocker loudly. Even though I had agreed to let Abel Wilks live there, I still felt as if I were the tenant. There was no reply, and I banged again. Barnaby had woken up, and romped along to the house with me. He now stood, barking, but wagging his tail too.

I heard the sound of footsteps, and the door was opened. Abel Wilks stood there. He was wearing corduroy trousers, and a blue shirt with the sleeves rolled up, showing his powerful arms. He wore no neckerchief, and his shirt was open almost to the waist. Obviously I had taken him by surprise.

'Oh, it's you, miss! Good day. Have you been knocking long? I'm sorry, I've been in the back. Come in.' Before I even stepped over the threshold, Barnaby rushed, growling, into the house. I had been prepared to find a mess in the kitchen, but such was not the case. The place was newly swept, and reasonably tidy.

'Good day,' I said. 'I didn't know you were already living here, until Mollie in the cottage told me.' There was just a hint of reproof in my voice, because although I had left her the key to hand over to him, I thought he would have let me know when he actually moved in.

'No. I'm sorry about that, miss. I've been so busy. I was going to write to you. Sit down.' He smiled at me as I did so, revealing his strong, white teeth. His

215

bold eyes were running over my face and figure in a somewhat disconcerting manner. 'They are repairing the mill,' he went on. 'Two men are working on it. I keep going along to see how they are getting on with things. After the harvest, the mill will be working.'

'Will you keep the hens?' I asked. 'They are good layers. Old Mollie in the cottage has been looking after them for me.'

'So she do say. I'll take the hens from you, miss.'

I stood hesitating, feeling that I should mention money now, but not really liking the idea. Abel Wilks must have read my thoughts.

'I'll give 'ee two sovereigns for the hens, and for the use of the furniture until you move what you require into the cottage. And when you do move your stuff, I'll give you help with it.'

It seemed a fair enough offer. 'Very well,' I said.

'I've been busy in the garden. There be plenty of vegetables.'

'Yes. You will reap the benefit of what I did earlier in the year,' I said with a smile.

'You be settled in the Hall, then, miss?' His manner became more familiar.

'Very settled,' I said.

'They do say the young Squire be without a wife.'

'Do they?' I was not going to gossip with him about what went on at Abinger Hall.

'I'll get the money.' He went into the parlour, and returned with a leather wallet in his hand. He was an odd type of man, I thought. There was a kind of raffishness about him, and he did not altogether seem to belong to the rural labouring class. Even if he did, there was no doubt he intended to get on in the world. He gave me the money, and his hand closed over mine. I was not really surprised, but I pulled my hand away quickly, as if I had not noticed his.

'Thank you,' I said briskly, standing up. 'The cottage will soon be ready, and then we can sort out the furniture. I take it you have none of your own?'

'No. I was in lodgings at Chollerford. The room above my shop there is not fit to live in. This suits me very well.'

Barnaby followed me to the door, growling and whining to himself.

'I'll see you before long then, I expect, miss.' Abel Wilks gave me a smile of such impudent boldness that I was quite discountenanced. I remembered that Dorothy wanted to look at the mill-house.

'You may see me again today,' I said. 'I have the Squire's young daughter with me, and she wants to see the mill-house. We will not be troubling you, though.'

'You don't trouble me, miss.'

I walked quickly back to Mollie's, with Barnaby beside me. There was no doubt Abel Wilks was a saucy fellow.

'Are you going to show me the mill?' asked Dorothy.

'Yes, we'll go for a walk there later on. And you can look at the mill-house, but someone else is living there now.'

'Who?'

'The new miller. A man called Abel Wilks.'

Some time later, I walked along to the mill-house with her, with Barnaby yapping and prancing about in front.

'Here it is,' I said. 'You may walk round the garden.' I took her hand, and we strolled round the now seemingly deserted place. I showed her the hens, and the vegetable garden.

When she had satisfied her curiosity about the mill-house, she went with me to the mill. The heavy door was open, and from within I could hear sounds of sawing and hammering.

'They're busy doing repairs,' I said. 'Nobody has worked the mill since before I was born.'

'All that long time ago,' said Dorothy, round-eyed. I could see that the green slime and weeds had been removed from the mill-wheel, in preparation for it to begin turning again.

'And the river goes right along, and

past our house,' said Dorothy wonderingly. I reflected that it had done her no harm to get some idea of how the cottagers lived. We walked back to Mollie's house, and I went with Dorothy to inspect the weeping willow tree in the garden.

'Look, it goes right down into the water,' she said wonderingly. 'Is it very old?'

'Very old, I believe.' Mollie had followed us, and was standing looking at the river.

'Did you hear about the Chollerford man who was drowned in the Sedge last month?' she asked. 'That makes two this year. Ah, there'll be another, you mark my words. You mark my words, my little maid,' she repeated, turning to Dorothy. The child looked somewhat frightened, and I was rather displeased with Mollie for talking thus in front of her. I laughed it off, and remarked that Charles should be coming with the dogcart any minute. He arrived shortly afterwards, and we got in and drove off, with much waving and many goodbyes to Mollie.

I knew that Dorothy had been very eager to visit her, so much so that she had postponed riding her new pony. However, we patted him and fussed over him on arriving back at Abinger Hall.

'Tomorrow morning you can ride him,' I said. At dinner that evening, I told Mr. Tregarth that the repairs were being carried out very well, and that Abel Wilks was now in the mill-house.

'Are you satisfied with things, then?' he enquired.

'Everything seems very satisfactory, sir. We had a very pleasant day, and Dorothy found much to interest her.' I glanced across at Miss Hepton. She had not spoken up to now, and appeared somewhat paler than usual.

'Unfortunately, Miss Hepton has had some rather bad news. She is going to have to leave us for a while,' remarked Mr. Tregarth.

'My aunt in London has been taken

ill. I've received a letter asking me to go there,' she explained.

'I'm sorry to hear that,' I said.

'Her housekeeper wrote the letter, so I had better go and see what is happening. I am afraid the tremendous task of sorting through all the stuff in the library is going to be held up now.' Miss Hepton sipped her wine thoughtfully, and looked at Mr. Tregarth.

'Don't worry about the books, Celia. The indexing will get done eventually,' he told her. From further remarks made at the dinner table, I gathered that he was seeing Miss Hepton off the following morning. She was being driven with her maid to Chollerford station, to take a train to the larger town of Chinwell, where she could get a connection to London.

'I hope you have a good journey,' I said to Miss Hepton. 'And I hope your aunt's condition is not too bad.'

'Thank you. I hope not,' she replied coldly. We left the table, and I went up to the nursery, reflecting that on the whole, my visit to Bramwell had been satisfactory. Then I thought about Miss Hepton having to go to London, and how much pleasanter it would be without her. I would dine with Howard Tregarth, with only Dorothy there, in future. We would talk together. He would not be able to ride with Miss Hepton, nor would she be closeted in the library with him.

I stood immersed in my own thoughts, and was quite surprised when I glanced at the clock, and realised that it was nearly time for me to visit the library and collect Dorothy. I could imagine how she had prattled to her father about the cottage and the mill-house, and Old Mollie. Well, he had not objected to her going there, and I was pleased about that. I tapped on the library door as usual, and as usual, Dorothy rushed to open it.

'I hear Dorothy has had a very interesting day,' her father said, smiling. 'Tomorrow, she will be out riding first thing, of course. It so happens that I shall be seeing Miss Hepton off on the train. Later on, though, there will be plenty of opportunity for me to see Dorothy on her new pony, I have no doubt.' There was an unmistakable warmth in his glance as he looked at me.

'We will look forward to seeing you at the stables, sir,' I said demurely. 'Come, Dorothy, say goodnight to your papa.'

10

I sat on Pete's back, and watched Dorothy being mounted on Toby. She had already ridden him a good deal, and by now she was thoroughly used to him, and he to her. Her father sat on his grey hunter, and waited until we were ready. I had somewhat hesitantly suggested to him that I thought I was now proficient enough on horseback to ride to the village, instead of having to be driven in the dogcart every time.

'If I am satisfied that you are capable, then you can ride, by all means. But first, I will accompany you and Dorothy to Bramwell.'

Naturally, she was delighted at the prospect, and the three of us set off along the drive in very high spirits. I felt so happy, just to have him with us. He seemed light-hearted too, talking and smiling, and keeping his horse at a steady pace. There were few people about on the narrow, winding lanes that morning. Because Howard Tregarth was with me, the birdsong sounded sweeter, the ripening corn looked more golden, and the poppies a brighter scarlet than ever before. We rode abreast most of the time, but if a waggon or carriage appeared we would go in single file, with Mr. Tregarth leading.

'By the way, I am giving a small dinner party this week,' he told me as we went along. 'As you know, I don't do a great deal of entertaining, because we are so busy here at the moment, but I am expecting a few guests on Friday; six, to be precise. I would like you to act as hostess, Miss Mountjoy.'

'Me? Oh, but I — ' I was on the point of saying that I couldn't, but he anticipated me.

'Please don't make lame excuses. Miss Hepton has been called away as you know, and I cannot entertain without a hostess. I see no reason why you should not be an excellent one.'

I was struck dumb at the thought. I would have to entertain guests in that muslin gown which I had made myself! How could I expect a man to understand these problems? While I was thinking desperately along these lines, Mr. Tregarth spoke again.

'Just be your natural self, Miss Mountjoy, and you will do very well. Should the need arise, I know that you are a competent pianist, and that you have an attractive singing voice. Oh, yes, I've heard you singing for Dorothy on occasions.'

'Papa, will I be coming down to dinner if Miss Mountjoy is?' asked Dorothy, who had been listening with interest. Her father seemed about to say no, and then appeared to have second thoughts.

'What do you think?' he asked me. 'Shall we let her come?' There was something flatteringly intimate about the way he was consulting me on this matter.

'I think she should,' I said boldly. 'Just this once. I think it will be a treat for her, and I'm sure she'll be good.'

'I will! I will!' came the gleeful cry from his daughter. So the matter was settled, and I tried to put my misgivings to one side. Mr. Tregarth wanted to see how the repairs to the mill were proceeding, but first we visited Mollie's cottage. She was quite overcome to find me at the door with Dorothy, and the Squire himself.

'Ah! It be Mr. Tregarth! Good day to 'ee, sir.' She bobbed a somewhat stiff curtsey in his direction. Barnaby rushed at me, barking, and I laughingly quietened him down.

'Well, so this is Mollie. And I presume this is your dog, Miss Mountjoy.'

Dorothy, full of importance, began to show her father how much she knew of the place. One of the workmen was still there, whitewashing the kitchen over the plastering which had been done.

'This be the last task, sir,' said the man, a trifle awed to find the Squire himself inspecting things.

'Good. I'll see how things are at the mill.' After a while the three of us walked along in the direction of the mill-house, with Barnaby frollicking ahead of us. I gathered from Mollie that he had made friends with Abel Wilks, and spent quite a lot of time at the mill-house.

'Look, Papa, this is the well where Miss Mountjoy had to get all her water from.'

'Did she indeed?' This remark was accompanied by a grin. 'I'm sure you don't miss that, Miss Mountjoy.'

'Not really,' I admitted. To myself I admitted a great deal more; that I didn't really miss the mill-house any longer. On this summer morning, with Howard Tregarth beside me, I was filled with happiness. Even the somewhat alarming prospect of acting as his hostess was for the time being put to one side. Abel Wilks was doing something to his waggon as we passed the mill-house. His horse was tethered, cropping the grass.

'Good day, Wilks,' called Mr. Tregarth.

'Good day, sir.'

'How are things proceeding at the mill, then?'

'Very well indeed. After the harvest, I'll be busy there.'

'I'm on my way to have a look at it now. I understand that you are willing to take Miss Mountjoy's furniture to the cottage for her. Send the bill in to my steward when you do so.'

'Very well, sir,' said Abel Wilks, after some hesitation. His swarthy face had reddened. I felt embarrassed, too. On the face of it, of course, Howard Tregarth was merely taking responsibility for moving me to other accommodation, having ended my tenancy at the millhouse. I wondered if there were not more to it, though. I would have offered to pay Wilks myself, even though he had hinted that helping me move was part of the bargain we had struck over the tenancy.

But I had no wish to be under an obligation to him. Clearly, the Squire was going to make sure himself that I was not.

Work was almost completed in the mill now. How clean and different it looked. I felt a passing sadness as we stood in the dim interior, with Dorothy's eyes wide with interest as she looked about her. So my father must have stood, and listened to the mill-race many a time, and perhaps sang to himself as he worked. And all these years it had stood idle . . .

'You look pensive,' remarked Mr. Tregarth, as we left the place.

'I was thinking how long it's been since anyone milled corn here,' I said. We started to walk back to Mollie's cottage.

'Too long. It will be a good thing to see the mill working again,' he said simply, and strangely enough, I found that I was inclined to agree with him. We said goodbye to Mollie some time later, and began our journey back to the

Hall, our horses going at a steady jogtrot.

'Well, sir,' I said, as we cantered into the stableyard, 'am I sufficiently proficient on horseback to make the journey to the cottage myself?' He had dismounted, and he helped me down. The touch of his hand on my arm made me catch my breath.

'I think we can say you are. And Dorothy is becoming a good horsewoman, too.' He helped his daughter down, and gave her a quick hug. Despite his somewhat stern manner, I suspected that he had a very affectionate nature. Walking into the house beside him, I was enfolded in a wonderful, half shy happiness. After luncheon he mentioned that if I could give him some help with the library indexing, he would be very grateful. 'It seems Miss Hepton will be detained in London for some time,' he added. I tried to conceal my pleasure on hearing that as best I could, and told him I would be pleased to help him.

'Perhaps if you could spare me an hour in the evenings after Dorothy's bedtime, that would be quite suitable. One does not like to stay indoors more than necessary when the weather is so fine.'

'I quite often do stay in after her bedtime,' I said. 'Dorothy and I get plenty of fresh air during the day.'

'Then I would be pleased to have your assistance any evening.'

I asked him about the menu for our guests that week, and he said he would leave it to me. 'See Cook, and tell her what you want.'

'I know what we'll have — ' began Dorothy, her eyes shining.

'You won't have anything,' said her father with mock severity. 'You won't be there, unless you behave yourself.'

For the rest of the day, I was in a dream of happiness. Abinger Hall was the most wonderful place in the world. Even though the repairs to Mollie's cottage were completed, and I could move my stuff there, it no longer seemed of any importance. I didn't want to spend one night, or even one hour away from the Hall and Howard Tregarth, if I could help it. That evening, after Dorothy was in bed, I smoothed my hair in front of the mirror, and went downstairs in my white lace blouse and black skirt. I tapped on the library door, and entered. Mr. Tregarth was not smoking, but there was the faintest smell of cigar smoke lingering in the room. I did not find it unpleasant. He was sitting at his leather covered desk, but rose, smiling, when I entered the room.

'This is very good of you, Miss Mountjoy. Be seated, and I will explain what I am trying to do. This is an excellent library, but it has been neglected, as everything else here has. There was an appalling amount of sheer rubbish to be got rid of, before I could start on anything else. It's a very slow business, I'm afraid. Some of the books are very old, and some are very interesting. This is not a task I can ask any of the servants to assist with.'

I sat opposite him at the desk, and for some time he talked about the books, and explained the system of indexing which he was doing with the assistance of Miss Hepton. Then we sat in companionable silence, while we worked, occasionally dipping our pens in the inkwell. Sometimes I glanced at him surreptitiously, and noticed the dark lock of hair which fell forward over his brow, and thought how the same thing happened with his daughter, when her plaits were loosened. I picked up a large tome about some expedition to a remote part of Africa, and found all the pages and the cover were stuck together.

'Look, sir,' I said. 'I don't know how this has happened. The book won't open at all.'

He glanced up. 'Let me see it.' I handed it across the desk, and he examined it carefully. 'It's been stuck together for a purpose,' he said slowly. He began to prize the leatherbound, gold-tooled back away from the pages. There was a tearing sound, and I gave a gasp of surprise. The pages had been neatly cut away in the centre, leaving a space in which objects could be concealed. He lifted out a folded piece of parchment, a small, black covered book, two miniatures in gilt frames, and a letter. He handed me the miniatures. One was of a young man, fair-haired and blue-eyed; the other of a dark-haired girl with large brown eyes, and a tender, childish mouth.

'Who are they?' I enquired.

'I've no idea. This is a diary.'

I began to feel rather embarrassed. Had I stumbled upon something which was a private, family matter? Thinking of the horrific findings in the Blue Room, I wished that Miss Hepton had found the book, or better still, Mr. Tregarth. But no, I had to be the one. I sat without speaking, while he looked through the diary.

'It was my uncle's,' he said slowly. 'I have found no other diaries of his. This one is nearly twenty years old. There are only scattered entries in it, and none after July of that year. There is one for July the twenty third which says: 'The evidence was removed; the cause of all the trouble left also'. That's puzzling, isn't it?'

Frowning, he turned over the next few pages. 'Three days later there is another entry: 'Everything has been attended to. What is done is done, now. Only I know the truth. May God forgive me'.'

Somehow, those words written years before, still seemed to breathe the long-ago anguish of Lionel Tregarth. His nephew picked up the letter and scrutinized it.

'It's written in French,' he said. 'I'm better at Italian. You have a look at it.'

It was a short letter, merely a page of faded writing. The address was a Paris one, and the date was March, eighteen sixty two.

''Dear Mr. Tregarth,'' I read out slowly — ''I am writing again to entreat you to help me. Please do not ignore this letter, as you have ignored my others. Even if you cannot forgive, I ask you to help me now, for pity's sake. I have no money; I have nothing. I have sold nearly all the bits of jewellery which I had. My heart is broken — the streets await me if you will not help me now. What is to become of us? You cannot be so cruel. Surely I have suffered enough; why should the innocent be punished? I can do nothing else but throw myself on your mercy. I am yours, Francoise Tregarth'.'

I looked across the desk. Even after twenty years, that despairing cry seemed to communicate itself to me.

'Who was Francoise Tregarth?' I asked.

'I'm afraid I don't know. The only thing I can think — ' Mr. Tregarth paused. 'There was talk that my cousin, Anthony, who died abroad, had run off and married some French dancer. He was my father's first cousin, I was just a child at the time.'

'Yes, I've heard something like that,' I admitted.

'Miss Hepton's father probably knew the whole story, but I doubt if she does. But she did tell me that my father became a recluse on account of the behaviour of his son, who died in France, after disgracing himself with some cheap little dancing girl. That was the version she heard, anyway. We've not been a very closely-knit family, or perhaps it may be truer to say Uncle Lionel didn't encourage any of his relatives to visit him. We lived in Cambridgeshire.' He looked thoughtful.

'This letter was written the same year as the diary,' I remarked.

Rather to my surprise, Howard Tregarth did not appear to want to keep all this to himself. He seemed both interested and intrigued, which I was myself. He opened out the piece of parchment.

'Well, this is a marriage certificate. Francoise D'arcy, and Anthony Tregarth, dated the September before. It

239

rather looks as if the unhappy creature who wrote that letter was his French wife, writing after his death.'

'Poor Francoise,' I said. 'I expect the miniatures are of them. I wonder if Mr. Tregarth gave her the help she was so desperate for.'

'I wonder too. There are no portraits of my cousin Anthony in the house, so I do not know if the miniature is of him. It seems more than likely that it is, though. I wonder how the marriage certificate came into my uncle's possession, and why he kept these things hidden away? We will never know.' He put the letter, the miniatures, and the marriage certificate carefully away in his desk. 'They always said he was an eccentric man,' he went on. 'I wonder what else we shall find hidden away?'

'Nothing, I hope,' I said quickly. He gave me an understanding look. He never mentioned the remains which I had discovered in the Blue Room, but I had a feeling he often thought about them, and wondered, as I did, who the woman had been.

'Well, I had better continue with my indexing,' I said. 'No more books with stuck pages, I hope.'

We worked on together, but somehow, I could not put the discovery of those things out of my mind. That despairing plea for help — was it possible that it had gone unheeded? However bitter Lionel Tregarth had been, surely he had not ignored that distracted cry?

Evidently the poor girl had not spoken English. What were the other entries in the diary? I pulled myself up sharply. It was certainly none of my business, and I had better not mention the matter again, unless Howard Tregarth did. I had an idea he was thinking about my discovery, too. The next hour or so passed uneventfully, but I indexed quite a large number of books. I found myself stifling a yawn, and Mr. Tregarth glanced up quickly.

'You've done quite enough for one evening,' he said. 'It's nearly ten o'clock.' I had not realised it was so late. It was strange how, after my discovery of the book with the hidden articles, we had both carried on working in silence. 'It has been very good of you to assist me like this, Miss Mountjoy, but I am sure you are tired now.'

I did not deny it. 'I will wish you goodnight, then,' he said, standing up. I rose, and for a moment we stood looking at each other in the lamplight.

'Good night, sir,' I said quietly. He walked to the door, and opened it for me.

'Good night, Miss Mountjoy,' he said again, almost abruptly. I went into the hall, took a candle from the table, and after lighting it, mounted the stairs. I wondered what Howard Tregarth's thoughts were, now that he was alone in the library. Was he thinking of me — or of those pathetic little relics which I had stumbled across? Why had Lionel Tregarth not destroyed them? Or, if he intended to keep them for some reason, why had he not merely locked them in a drawer? But then, everyone seemed to agree that he had been a very eccentric man.

Why had Howard Tregarth talked about them to me, though, instead of treating the matter as a private concern?

The following day, Dorothy rode with me in the grounds, and we went past the disused quarry. 'I know a secret about this place,' she announced.

'You've been forbidden to come here,' I told her. 'You are not to play in this quarry.'

'I don't — not now. But I know that under those big stones and things there's a door that leads somewhere. I've peeped through the spaces between the stones, and seen it. Will there be something behind that door?'

'Of course not,' I said sharply. Had Dorothy, after all, caught wind that something had been found behind the stonework in the Blue Room? No, I did not think so. Rosie would not face the prospect of dismissal, even for the delight of telling Dorothy such a horrible story, and a true one at that. That child was just exceptionally curious.

'You must keep away from it,' I told her severely. 'Your father would be very angry if he knew you had been in the old quarry. He would be angry with me, too.'

'I won't go in again. I promise. Don't tell Papa.'

'Very well. Now come on, let's get away from here. It's going to be very hot this afternoon.' To my surprise I saw her father on horseback too, riding towards us.

'I have a plan for today,' he announced gaily. 'I propose that we have a picnic luncheon by the river.'

Dorothy was enchanted with the idea, which truth to say, so was I. How delightful life at Abinger Hall was without the presence of Miss Hepton. Later on, in sun-bonnets and muslin dresses, Dorothy and I set off for our picnic. It was very informal; Mr. Tregarth had said that we didn't know the spot we wanted until we found it, and he had dismissed the idea of having the food brought out to us, so he carried the luncheon basket himself.

'We'll have to find a nice, shady place,' he said. 'It's extremely hot. I hope you don't mind if I remove my jacket.' He did so, which I could understand, as Dorothy and I were overheated in our thin dresses. We found an idyllic spot for a picnic, under a tree by the river.

'What did Cookie put in for us?' was the inevitable question from Dorothy. 'I'm hungry.'

With a smile, her father handed the basket to me. There were chicken legs, dainty sandwiches, and mutton patties. There was also cake, fruit, glasses, and a bottle of wine, and one of ginger beer. I spread the little cloth out on the grass, and set out the plates and glasses. Soon all three of us were munching happily. We had to face some slight irritation from midges and other insects, but this did not mar the enjoyment of the occasion. It was intoxicating to be so close to Howard Tregarth.

'Papa, take us on the river,' begged Dorothy, when the meal was over.

'Not today, Dorothy.'

'It's too hot to play with my ball, Papa.'

'Yes, and it's too hot for me to think of rowing you! Make a nice long daisy chain, and put it round Miss Mountjoy's neck.'

She went off to find some choice specimens. We both sat without speaking; the spell of warm summer days seemed as if they would never end now. On all sides was the innocence of nature at its best; it helped to fade the memory of the discovery in the Blue Room.

A soft breeze fluttered the leaves on the trees, and lifted up the corners of the tablecloth. It blew Howard Tregarth's hair away from his temples, too. Sitting together on the grass, I felt a closeness between us that seemed to need no words. He moved his position very slightly, and I became aware that his hand was touching mine, but with a touch so light, so unobtrusive, that it almost might not have been. If I moved my finger, just fractionally, the contact would end. We sat there, still silent, while all around us the birds sang in the trees, and the dragonflies hovered and darted over the glinting water of the Sedge.

For a few moments it was a fairytale world of blue skies and sunshine; of a hand just barely touching mine, and glorious happiness welling up inside me. Would he say something about his feelings? Would he kiss me? No, that was unlikely with Dorothy around, even though she was engrossed in picking flowers.

'You are quite happy about the dinner party, I trust?' he said.

'Well, sir, I think I've decided on a suitable menu, and I will do my best to entertain your guests.'

'And there is nothing troubling you?'

I hesitated. 'My gown is very simple, I'm afraid,' I said slowly.

''Vanity, thy name is woman'', he quoted, with a smile.

'It's not vanity, I can assure you,' I said quickly. 'It is that I am afraid I will not look correct, acting as hostess.'

'I think I understand, now that you put it that way,' he said quietly. 'You always look very nice to me, if I may say so. I may be able to help you, though — ah, here is Dorothy.'

She appeared with two daisy chains, which she put round our necks with great ceremony. The three of us spent nearly the whole day together. We went back to the house for tea, and then I repaired to the schoolroom with Dorothy, and insisted on her doing some lessons, for as I pointed out, she'd had a very easy day. That evening, as I had promised, I again went down to help Mr. Tregarth in the library. As soon as I entered the room, he produced a large parcel, and handed it to me. 'Concerning your worry about a suitable gown,' he said, 'I have one here which may well fit you. It was made for my late wife, but she never wore it. She was too ill.'

'Oh,' I said, somewhat taken aback. He took the gown out of the parcel, and held it up. It was plain, which meant that it was still fashionable, and beautifully cut. It was made of silk, and in the softest, loveliest shade of rose-pink imaginable.

'It's beautiful,' I said. 'May I go and try it on now?'

'Certainly. Take it away with you — and come down in it.'

I hurried off upstairs, and into my room. Hastily I removed my blouse and skirt, and slipped the gown carefully over my head. I would need help with some of the buttons, but it would have to do for now. I was slim, but it was close fitting on me. It was just about the right length. I twirled round in front of the looking glass. The colour suited me perfectly. There was no doubt that this dress would give me confidence. I could see no reason why I should not borrow it for the evening. I went downstairs, and entered the library again.

Mr. Tregarth caught his breath when he saw me, and coloured up. Then the sudden flush faded, and left him looking drained and white. There was no doubt that the sight of me in that gown moved him painfully.

'You look . . . utterly charming,' he said, speaking with a visible effort. 'My wife, Matilda, was fair. She was about your size, although towards the end, she became very — ' he broke off, as it was clearly too upsetting for him to talk about her physical deterioration. 'You will wear it, then?' he asked.

'It's beautiful! But are you sure you don't mind?'

'I would not have suggested it if I did.'

'It is very kind of you to let me borrow it.'

'Borrow it? I had not thought of that. No, Miss Mountjoy, it is yours to have, if you wish. Now don't put that look on your face, please.'

'Thank you very much, sir,' I said. 'As for keeping it, well, I shall have to think about that. But certainly I will wear it at the dinner party.'

★   ★   ★

'What a charming young lady your daughter is growing into, to be sure,' said Mrs. Boldwood to Mr. Tregarth. She patted Dorothy's head. Dorothy was on her best behaviour, only speaking when she was spoken to, but that was quite often, as the guests seemed to be going out of their way to make her feel important. Mrs. Boldwood was there without her husband, who had developed a chill, in spite of the warm weather. She had with her her daughter Kate, who must have been about my age, and her son, Roger, who was a few years older. There was also a Mr. Appleyard, and his wife, Clara. They were both in their late twenties, and, I gathered, had not lived in the district for long. I had arranged the flowers myself, taking care that they were done quite as well as Miss Hepton could have done them. The dinner was excellent, and there were many compliments from the guests.

I knew that my borrowed gown became me well, but I was a little surprised to find that the company seemed to accept me as the hostess, in Miss Hepton's absence. Naturally, they enquired about her, but although they knew that I was Dorothy's governess, they did not make me feel out of place. In fact, I soon had a feeling that Roger Boldwood was rather interested in me. When I led the ladies out of the dining room, he glanced after me admiringly.

'Play the piano for the company,' begged Dorothy, when we were in the drawing room.

'The company may not wish me to. I will play if they do,' I said.

'Perhaps later — when the gentlemen

join us,' suggested Mrs. Boldwood. 'Let us just sit and talk. Kate is friendly with Miss Hepton, but at the present time, I'm afraid she is rather bored.'

'I shan't be bored when the hunting season starts,' said her daughter. She laughed impishly, and I realized what an attractive young woman Kate Boldwood was. She had a warmer personality than Miss Hepton, I thought. No doubt a mutual love of horses had drawn them together. Mrs. Appleyard was a sweet, quiet woman, not particularly fashionable, but with a very agreeable, gentle manner, which gave her a certain charm, despite the fact that her appearance was so ordinary.

'My elder sister is a governess,' she said, rather unexpectedly. 'When she did not get married, naturally, my parents expected her to stay at home. But Marion is very independent, and off she went, in spite of all the opposition at home.' She gave me an encouraging smile as she said this.

'One of Kate's governesses was very similar to your sister, I should think,' said Mrs. Boldwood. 'She came from an excellent family. However, in the end, a very determined young gentleman took her away from us. I'm afraid this does happen to these pretty and charming governesses. You must guard your Miss Mountjoy, Dorothy.'

I felt a bit embarrassed, although the remark was made in the nicest way. Dorothy did not quite understand what Mrs. Boldwood meant.

'Would you like to recite for the ladies?' I asked her. 'The poem about the squirrels and birds, which you recite so nicely.'

'Yes! Do let us hear it,' cried Miss Boldwood.

Accordingly, Dorothy stood and recited it in a clear little voice. She had an expressive face, and delivered her lines well. Her audience clapped appreciatively, and I felt extremely proud of her. I knew that her father would have been delighted, if he had seen her. She gave a funny little curtsey at the sound of the applause, aware that she was the centre of attention.

'My, it's a very different place from what it was with poor Lionel,' said Mrs. Boldwood, shaking her head. 'We were always friendly with the colonel, but the old Squire, as they called him, was a very difficult man. He cut himself off completely from society. He tolerated Celia's father — and Celia, if it came to that. But I don't think anyone got really close to him. Young Howard seems to want to get the place as it was at one time, which is a splendid idea, I think.'

'Yes, Celia said he was determined to have a harvest supper this year, so that should be something to look forward to,' said her daughter.

'You may not be invited,' remarked Mrs. Boldwood, laughing. 'Ah, here come the gentlemen. They have not lingered as long as they sometimes do.'

Howard Tregarth entered the room with the other two men.

'Your daughter has been entertaining us,' said Mrs. Boldwood. 'She recited a poem beautifully, didn't she, ladies?' There was a chorus of assent, and he looked very gratified.

'I am afraid it is bedtime now,' I said, ringing the bell. 'I can't be with you tonight, Dorothy, so we will say our good-nights here.'

This she did, with considerable ceremony, kissing everyone in the room. After she had gone, all the guests remarked on her charm and brightness.

'Now, Miss Mountjoy, do play for us,' suggested Mrs. Appleyard. 'My husband can sing.'

'Certainly I will,' I said. 'If the company wish it.'

It seemed the company did, and together we sorted out some music. Mr. Appleyard had a very fine tenor voice, which made playing for him a delight. Everyone clapped wildly, and then Mr. Tregarth suggested that Mr. Appleyard and I should sing a duet, while he accompanied us.

'We haven't practised,' I said, somewhat dubiously.

'We will all improve as we go on,' said Mr. Tregarth, who seemed quite set on the idea. Before long I found myself singing with Mr. Appleyard, and the audience were most appreciative.

'I can't do anything, but I love other people to do things,' remarked Mrs. Boldwood. 'Kate and Roger are the same, I'm afraid.'

'Really, Mama, I have been known to play a very good tune with spoons,' protested her son. We had a footman who taught me years ago.'

He was as charming and jolly as his sister, and I knew he was becoming interested in me. He rarely took his eyes off me. The evening passed off splendidly, and when it was time for the guests to depart, I took the ladies into the guest room, where they had left their wraps. Then, begging to be excused a moment, I hurried off to the night nursery, to make sure that my charge was all right. She was sound asleep. As I returned to the guest room, I caught a snatch of conversation through the half opened door.

' . . . yes, it's been most unpleasant for them . . . the skeleton of an unknown woman, Howard was most upset . . . ' That was Mrs. Boldwood's voice. Then I heard her say: 'Miller's daughter? Are you sure, Kate? She has the bearing of a gentlewoman.'

'I would have thought so, too.' That was Mrs. Appleyard.

I coughed somewhat self consciously before entering the room. I knew well enough that they had been discussing me, but they immediately chattered brightly of other things. Mr. Tregarth and I both waved the guests farewell; not before Roger Boldwood had said that he hoped they would be seeing me at Tyzanger Grange before long.

'It's been a wonderful evening, and thank you for being such a splendid hostess,' said Mr. Tregarth, as we turned back into the house. All was silent now; the servants were in bed.

'I have enjoyed it very much,' I said. We walked into the hall together. He lit a candle in a silver candlestick, and handed it to me in silence. Then he took one for himself. Together we mounted the stairs, our shadows growing enormous in the candlelight. We did not speak. I knew that his room was not in the nursery wing of the house, like mine.

'Good night, Miss Mountjoy,' he said, when we reached the landing.

'Good night, sir.' For a moment he paused, as if he would say more, but with a quick smile, he went silently off. I walked along to my room. It was late, and those deserted corridors had an unpleasantly eerie appearance in the candlelight. I was thankful when I had passed the Blue Room. The conversation which I had overheard came back to me. So his friends thought that I had the bearing of a gentlewoman. I smiled bitterly to myself. The plain fact remained that I was not a girl from a good family, wishing to play at being independent, but knowing that I could always go home when the game palled. I was but a miller's daughter, however surprising it may seem to some people.

11

'Well, my love,' said Old Mollie, 'and when be you coming to spend the night with me?' We looked round at the bedroom, which now contained some of my furniture. The little table and the bookcase so dear to my mother, the photograph of my father, my bed and chest-of-drawers; all the beloved old objects had been brought from the mill-house by Abel Wilks.

He stood in the bedroom doorway. 'Yes,' he said, with an impudent grin. 'When are you?' He would get familiar with me if he could, I knew, and yet, he was such a bouncy, good-natured fellow that it was hard to find him really offensive.

'I can't really say that, Mollie. I've given so much of my time to Dorothy that she's come to expect it,' I said. 'And the young lady who lives at the

Hall is away at the moment, so Dorothy really has no one but me just now. But I know that all is ready here if I decide to come any time.'

Although I was speaking the truth, the real reason why I was in no hurry to take a day off and spend it at the cottage, was, quite simply, because I was hopelessly in love with Howard Tregarth, and had no desire to leave Abinger Hall. I knew that I would have to spend a day with Mollie before long, though; it was only right. I had completed my furniture transaction with Abel Wilks, to our mutual satisfaction. We went downstairs into the kitchen, where Mollie celebrated my removal by making a pot of Earl Grey tea, something which she did not drink every day.

My twentieth birthday had been the week previous, and Dorothy had insisted on having a big fuss about it. We'd had a special dinner, with an iced cake with candles for me.

'Make a wish,' Dorothy had said, just

as I had to her. And I had made one; a hopeless wish, I knew, but I had wished it with all my heart. Afterwards, Dorothy had presented me with a box of finest lawn handkerchieves, trimmed with lace, and her father had given me a lovely rosewood workbox. The three of us had sat in the drawing room afterwards. We had played games, and Dorothy had recited, and then I had played a duet on the piano, with her father. It had been a wonderful evening.

No less enjoyable had been the evening I had spent at Tyzanger Grange. I knew that Mr. Tregarth sometimes dined there with Miss Hepton, thus flouting convention somewhat, as she was unchaperoned. But this time the invitation card named me as the person expected to accompany him. And for me not to go would be the height of discourtesy. Accordingly, I was driven there one lovely, warm, summer evening, with Howard Tregarth sitting opposite me in the carriage. I was, perforce, wearing the pink gown again.

As he had indicated that he wished me to keep it, I felt I could scarcely do otherwise.

We had a very pleasant evening at the Boldwoods' attractive old house. Tyzanger Grange had never been allowed to fall into disrepair, like Abinger Hall. After dinner we played charades. There were about a dozen other guests there, and I might have felt a little out of my depth, but people clearly accepted me because the Boldwoods did, and because I was with Howard Tregarth. Roger Boldwood more than accepted me. He was very interested in me, and obviously hoping to see me again. The forthcoming harvest supper at Abinger Hall was the subject of much interest.

Mr. Boldwood, now recovered from his chill, said that he could remember when the Hunt Ball was held at Abinger Hall.

'It may well be held there again,' said Mr. Tregarth, smiling. I suddenly realized how much more often he smiled these days, and how much happier he seemed than when I had first set foot in Abinger Hall. This would all end if Miss Hepton arrived back, I thought, when, after a delightful evening, we said our goodbyes, and got into the brougham. Apparently, though, her aunt was very ill indeed, so she could scarcely be left.

'Have you enjoyed yourself?' asked Howard Tregarth, as our carriage moved away.

'I have indeed. The Boldwoods are such a charming family.'

'Do you like the son, Roger?'

'Very much, sir.' I said this artlessly.

'H'm. I think he's a bit of a lady killer, personally.'

'Really? I find him charming.'

'I suppose a number of young ladies would. I rather think he would flirt with anyone. You do not strike me as being the flirtatious type, Miss Mountjoy.'

'As far as that is concerned, I had not thought what type I am.'

'Perhaps you have not yet had much experience with the opposite sex.'

'Perhaps not.'

'I must warn you, then, not to take any heed of young Boldwood, as I can see he is greatly taken with you. I know that you are alone in the world, and I do not want any unhappiness brought upon you while you are at Abinger Hall.'

'I am grateful to you for your concern, sir.' I thought to myself how little he knew that I was already unhappy. Yet I was madly happy, too, at the same time. As for being attracted to Roger Boldwood — how could I be, when my heart was already engaged?

'There is a certain type of young man who is not above trifling with — ' he broke off.

'Not above trifling with . . . whom?' I asked, turning my full gaze upon him.

'I mean, Roger Boldwood could quite easily get the wrong impression about you. He may not understand how highly you are regarded at Abinger Hall,' he finished, somewhat lamely.

'I fully understand, sir,' I said quietly.

'I am merely your daughter's governess. No doubt you mean that he may think it rather amusing to flirt with me, as he would not do with a girl in his sister's position. I am not likely to lose my head over him, though.'

'I did not mean that at all.'

'What did you mean, then?'

'I meant that I shall see he does not trifle with you, whatever his reasons.' His face set in much harder lines. Was he merely protecting me from being taken advantage of; a rich young man could do that very easily with a poor governess. Or was it plain, ordinary jealousy on his part? By mutual consent we changed the subject, and I remarked that I was planning to have my furniture moved into Mollie's cottage that week.

And now it was moved in, and Barnaby was flopping lazily about, wagging his tail, and Mollie was pouring out cups of tea, and wondering when I would be spending a night there. Strange that it would have meant so much to me a few months ago, and now it meant so little.

'They say there's going to be a big harvest supper at the Hall,' remarked Abel Wilks. 'With dancing and drinking, and merrymaking. I suppose you dance, miss?'

'Yes, I dance,' I said, with a smile.

'I'll see you there, no doubt,' he went on, his fine, dark eyes gleaming with anticipation. After he left us, Old Mollie asked me what I thought of him.

'I don't think anything, really,' I said. 'He's moved the furniture for me, and he seems a good-natured person to have as a neighbour.'

'You like the young Squire, don't you?'

'Yes.' I did not add to that. There was no need to, with Mollie.

'He'll not marry his daughter's governess,' she said.

'Do you think that knowing that is going to alter my feelings?'

'No. But 'ee could have Abel Wilks — and many's the maid who would envy you.'

'I don't doubt it.'

I thought about what she said, as I rode back to Abinger Hall. I was living very much in the present, and it was a kind of wonderful, waking dream. I was seeing so much of Howard Tregarth, even though most of the time, Dorothy was with us too. If only I knew what his true feelings were towards me! But whatever they were, Mollie's words had struck a note of common sense.

The harvesting was proceeding in the fields around. With plodding pace the horses were pulling the reaping machines along, leaving the fallen corn in little heaps, the quantity of a sheaf. Most of the binders in the field were women. I could see them in their cotton bonnets and brown field overalls, binding the sheaves of fallen corn. They wore gloves to protect their hands, and I knew that they had been binding since dawn, and would go on until dusk. It had been sheep washing time when I had first made the journey to Abinger Hall. Then it was shearing time, and

Dorothy had laughed to see all the sheep looking so funny. And now it was harvest time.

Preparations for the harvest supper went on. The dry, sunny weather seemed as if it would never end. I spent a night with Mollie, because I felt it was only right to do so, and she was very pleased. Abel Wilks saw my horse tethered there, and came to the cottage with some trout he had caught in the river.

I thought the best plan was to adopt a pleasant, cheerful manner towards him, and disregard his bold eyes, and the various hints he dropped suggesting that we might have a closer relationship.

Another man was displaying interest in me. Roger Boldwood had been to Abinger Hall alone, on one pretext or another. One day he had lunched with Mr. Tregarth, I knew, but I had not been asked to join them. The shooting season had begun, and I supposed there would be a good deal of activity among the men in the county. Mr. Tregarth had consulted me about the harvest supper, and I had made suggestions. I thought that sandwiches and cakes should be provided in the early afternoon, so that the villagers with young families could enjoy themselves. There would be ale and cider for the men, and tea for their wives, and lemonade for the children. In the evening we would have a ball and supper, and those of the villagers who were free could join in.

'Well! You seem to have very decided views on how the harvest home should be celebrated,' said Mr. Tregarth, with a smile.

'You asked me if I had any ideas.'

'Yes, and the suggestions you have made sound very sensible to me,' he admitted. 'We haven't got room in the house for too many people to dance, though.'

'It will have to be partly indoors and partly outdoors, then,' I said. 'That won't matter. If it's a fine night, the music will sound outside, with all the doors and windows open. And if the floor gets a bit crowded, it won't matter anyway. It's an occasion for mixing and being friendly.'

'Yes,' said Howard Tregarth. 'An occasion for rejoicing.'

From then on it was all preparations for the harvest supper. Abel Wilks had promised to bring Mollie in his waggon. I had visited the dressmaker at Chollerford again, and had the style of the gown which Mr. Tregarth had given me copied as closely as possible in cream taffeta. I was very pleased with the result. Dorothy and I had been busy making chains of coloured paper to hang in the hall, together with garlands of green foliage, and a fine array of corn dollies made by the buxom Rosie, who was an expert in the art. The week the harvest supper was to be held, Mr. Tregarth received a letter from Miss Hepton, saying that her aunt was much better, and that she was coming back to Abinger Hall the day before the supper. She asked to be met in Chollerford.

One thing I was certain of now, whatever Mr. Tregarth's feelings were towards me, he was not in love with Miss Hepton. He arranged for her to be met, but, as he told me, he was far too busy that day to meet her himself. Even so, I did not relish the prospect of her return. When Dorothy was told, her naive remark was: 'Oh, it's so nice, with the three of us.'

I was pleased that we were in the nursery, and her father did not hear it. What she said found an echo in my own heart. Things would not be the same with Miss Hepton there. For one thing, she would immediately assume the position of hostess. I would be nobody again. I had looked forward to the harvest supper so much, too.

Miss Hepton appeared at dinner the day she returned. Her gaze turned to me with a hostile look. I asked politely after her aunt's health.

'She is much improved, but still very poorly,' was her reply. 'Tell me all that has happened in my absence,' she said to Mr. Tregarth.

'Very little, really,' he said. 'As you know, the big event is tomorrow. That is why we are having such a simple meal tonight. The servants will be busy from dawn tomorrow — they have been very busy today, too.'

'And why shouldn't they be? Yes, you are right about the dinner being a simple meal, Howard.' She was not in a good mood, that was plain. In fact, the atmosphere at the dinner table seemed strained. I had promised to go down to the servants' hall after dinner, to assist in the preparations for the following day. Mr. Tregarth had said it was not necessary, but I said that I had promised Rosie and Simkins that I would help them decorate the hall, ready for the dancing.

'I shall come too, then,' he said. 'You must go to bed early tonight, I'm afraid, Dorothy. No games in the library.' She didn't mind, as she knew she would be up late the following night.

'Who is coming to the supper?'

enquired Miss Hepton. 'I don't mean the villagers, of course.'

'The Boldwoods, the Appleyards, the Treachers — all the families you know, in fact. And we have engaged some first-rate musicians from Chollerford. The villagers have their own fiddlers and flautists, of course, so there should be plenty of music.'

'It's just as well I'm back in time for all this, then,' remarked Miss Hepton. 'You will need a proper hostess. But tonight I am tired, so I will rest in my room. Good night.' She rose somewhat haughtily, and left the table.

'Good night. Come along, Dorothy,' I said. Mr. Tregarth did not speak, but when I glanced at him, I could see his face was white with anger. He was not angry with me, but, I guessed, with Miss Hepton. I knew then that things were going to come to a head. She had left her aunt, still very ill, and travelled back to Abinger Hall. I suspected this was to find out what was going on. It was more than likely that news had reached her that I had taken over certain tasks in her absence. She assumed she would immediately relieve me of them, as of right.

I went to the nursery with Dorothy, and after she was in bed, I repaired to the servants' hall, where Rosie and Simkins were arguing about the decorations, which they had spread out on the table. Simkins produced a step ladder, and the three of us went into the great entrance hall of the house.

'I shall arrange the flowers first thing tomorrow morning,' I said.

I was determined to do that. I had helped to plan all this, and Miss Hepton was not going to push in and interfere now. The harvest supper as such meant nothing to her, anyway. She had no time for the villagers. Howard Tregarth appeared in the hall, while we were busy, and said that he wanted a word with me in private.

'Very well, sir,' I said, putting down a corn dolly. I followed him to the library, where he bade me be seated.

'I want you to act as hostess at the harvest supper, Miss Mountjoy,' he said.

'But sir, Miss Hepton said she would be doing that now.'

'I did not say so, though. I am the master here.' I sat without speaking, feeling painfully uncomfortable. What would happen at the harvest supper ball?

'But what will people think?' I said at last. 'I know I have acted as hostess once or twice in her absence, but after all, I am only your daughter's governess — '

'There is no 'only' about it,' he said shortly. 'I am well aware what you are in this house — and what you have done for Dorothy. Miss Hepton has lived here for many years, because of an arrangement between my late uncle and her father. My uncle did not leave a will, and I inherited the entire estate as my uncle's next-of-kin. Naturally I considered it would have been discourteous of me to ask Miss Hepton to give up her apartments here as soon as I took possession of Abinger Hall. And I admit that in many ways she was very helpful to me, having lived here so long, and being well known in the neighbourhood. I was grateful to her, naturally, but I always knew it was a state of affairs which could not continue indefinitely. She has been away several weeks, during which time she has written to me, and I have replied to her letters. Now she has come back, she assumes that everything will be exactly the same as it was before she went away. I did not like her high-handed manner at the dinner table this evening.'

I had not liked it, either, but I was very taken aback that Mr. Tregarth had talked to me about it. I was on the point of saying that surely Miss Hepton was the one to approach about the matter, but he anticipated me by saying that he was going to speak plainly to her the following day.

'I know she has been travelling, and is tired this evening,' he went on. 'We will get back to the hall now, and finish the decorations.'

We did so, but I still had misgivings about the morrow. I felt elated because Howard Tregarth had confided in me, and had confirmed the servants' gossip which Dorothy had repeated to me, about there being no will. It seemed quite plain, too, that as far as he was concerned Miss Hepton could leave Abinger Hall as soon as she pleased. While I was thinking thus, word came from a maid that Abel Wilks was at the back of the house with his waggon, and wished to see me urgently.

'Send him in here, then,' said Mr. Tregarth, coolly. 'Can you think why he should wish to see you tonight?'

'I cannot, sir,' I said. He would not come to Abinger Hall like this unless it was about a matter of some importance, I reflected. Within the next few minutes, I knew what it was.

'Miss Mountjoy! Good evening, sir. I've come on account of Old Mollie. She's been taken very ill, and is begging to see you — and she wants a magistrate as well. I'll take 'ee in the waggon with me — '

'Oh, dear!' I gasped. 'Poor Mollie!'

'Someone from the village is staying with her — a woman called Susan Grey.'

'And you say she wants a magistrate?' asked Mr. Tregarth.

'That's what she says, sir.'

'It's very good of you to come, Wilks. However, it will not be necessary for you to drive Miss Mountjoy to the cottage. I am a magistrate, and as the poor old woman is asking for one, I will take Miss Mountjoy there.'

We set off behind Abel Wilks' waggon. It seemed an interminable drive. We did not speak much; I was too upset over Mollie to want to talk. I was thinking about the harvest supper, too. I might not be able to attend it after all, in which case Mr. Tregarth would be thankful for Miss Hepton to act as hostess. Abel Wilks drove straight past the mill-house, and up to Mollie's cottage. Barnaby ran out, barking and leaping about as soon as he saw us. His dusty pawmarks covered my dress in no time. A gaunt looking, middle-aged woman appeared at the door when she heard the commotion. It was Susan Grey, one of the few villagers on calling terms with Mollie. I knew that Mollie had helped nurse her mother many years before, and Susan Grey was fond of her, and could be relied upon to do what she could.

'I'm glad you came — ' she broke off when she saw the Squire, and dropped a quick curtsey. 'Old Mollie is very ill,' she added.

'Yes,' I said. I had a dreadful, choked feeling. The woman led the way upstairs, and I followed her. Howard Tregarth came behind me, and Abel Wilks brought up the rear. I don't think Mollie had ever had so many visitors at once before. We went into the cramped, untidy little room.

'Mollie!' I said, and knelt down beside the bed. 'It's Clare! I'm here.

The Squire is here, too.' How desperately ill she looked. Her face was grey; her white hair an unkept tangle, and she was breathing with difficulty.

'Clare,' she gasped, after several attempts to speak. Her sunken eyes were upon me. 'I — must — tell — you something. Give me my Bible — I need — a magistrate — '

'I've brought a flask of brandy with me,' said the Squire, in a low voice. 'Give her a drop. And Wilks, send my coachman for the doctor, will you? I am a magistrate,' he added gently, to Mollie.

Susan Grey poured some brandy into a cup, and held it to the old woman's lips. She swallowed a few mouthfuls, and some dribbled unheeded down her chin. Abel Wilks came quietly back into the room.

'Where is her Bible?' asked Mr. Tregarth. 'I think she wants to swear an oath. Do you want to take an oath to tell the truth, Mollie?' he asked. The old woman nodded, a Bible was produced, and under his guidance she roused herself, and took the oath. Then she began to speak, slowly and jerkily, in front of a magistrate and three other witnesses.

'Twenty years ago — yes — twenty years ago — Jennie Mountjoy lived in the mill-house, and her son had died, and her daughter-in-law had a baby. I delivered it, a weak, sickly girl. It was baptised Clare, the same day. And that same day — no, it was night, a masked man came to my door, and asked me to accompany him to a confinement. He said I would come to no harm; he asked me to trust him, and said I would be well paid, but I must tell no one about it.'

She paused a moment, and then continued: 'I didn't want to go at first, but he begged me again to trust him. He showed me the carriage he had come in. He said I must be blindfolded, but that no harm would come to me. He swore it. He swore it and gave me a sovereign. So I got into the carriage.

The coachman was masked, too. As the carriage moved off, the man blindfolded me. He never spoke as we drove along, except to tell me not to worry.' She stopped speaking for a moment.

'Go on, Mollie,' I said softly.

'When the carriage stopped at last, the man helped me down. I was still blindfolded. I knew that I was walking on grass, and then I was taken along somewhere where I could hear our footsteps echoing. Then I was taken up some steps. Ten steps, I counted them. Then I was led along, and up some more steps. I began to count them, but the two men hurried me too quickly. We stopped going up steps, and the men led me along. A door was opened and closed, and my blindfold was removed. The man who had given me the sovereign stood there. The coachman had gone. I was in a room, with a young woman lying there on a bed, in the last stages of labour.

''Deliver her,' said the man. 'And when you have, ring that bell.' He left the room. There was a good fire in the hearth, with a large kettle on it. There were towels, basins; everything I would need. The poor girl moaned, and cried out to me, but she did not speak, except for strange mutterings which I could not understand.'

Mollie stopped talking, and gasped for breath. The room was silent; the four of us were grouped round her bed, listening. She indicated that she must have another drink of brandy. After a few minutes rest, she went on again, but her voice was weaker.

'At last, I delivered her of a girl. I showed her the baby. The young woman had two silver bracelets on her wrist. She removed one, and slipped it on the baby's tiny wrist. The child was well enough, but the mother seemed very ill. I thought that she should have a doctor. I rang the bell, but it was too late. The girl died before anyone came.'

The voice stopped again. I was fascinated by what she was saying, and the other three appeared to be, as well.

After a while, she went on talking.

'The man came back into the room. He was still masked. I had wrapped the baby in a blanket, and put it at the foot of the bed. The man asked me if I would lay out the young woman. By then I felt I'd had enough of that house, but in the end I agreed to. After I had done so, he asked me to wait a few minutes. After he had left the room, I tried the door, but it was locked. I felt afraid. I was going to ring the bell again, but the man returned, with the masked coachman.

The man had a little bag, with some sovereigns in it. He said if I would take the child, and say nothing of what had happened that night, then I should have the money. He said I could do what I liked with the baby, as long as I took it away. I was afraid, and I did not want to stay there any longer. I picked up the sleeping babe, and they blindfolded me again. The two men led me down all those steps again, and back along the way I had come.' Here Mollie stopped speaking, and I did not think she would be able to say any more. But once again she rallied, and went on with her story.

'I was helped into the coach, and driven along. It was just becoming light when the blindfold was removed, and I was back at the door of the cottage. I came in with the baby, put it into bed, and fell asleep beside it. When I woke up, somebody was knocking very loudly at the door. I got up, thinking it had all been a dream, but no, the baby was there, still asleep. It was Jennie Mountjoy at the door. She was crying, and said that her daughter-in-law's baby had died in the night. She said the poor girl was still asleep, and how could she tell her what had happened when she woke up? And then I told her about the masked men, and the birth, and showed her the baby. I said why not take it, and pretend it was theirs. Both babies were black-haired; why not let this unwanted child bring them joy at the mill-house? At first she wouldn't agree, but I carried the child to the mill-house. I said I would bury the little dead one for her. She was upset at the idea, but there wasn't much time to think about it. I . . . gave . . . you to her, Clare, and took the dead baby away — '

'Mollie!' I cried, suddenly realizing the full significance of the story she had told us. I looked round. The eyes of the other three were fixed on me. I felt as though my life had collapsed round me like a pack of cards. 'It's not true,' I said. 'If I'm not Clare Mountjoy, who am I?'

'I don't know,' came the weary voice from the bed. 'I took 'ee for a few gold coins, as the price of my silence. I kept the bracelet — it's in the trunk. The key be under my pillow.'

Mr. Tregarth seemed to have recovered from the first shock of her words.

'Where did you bury the other baby?' he asked gently. 'Tell me, Mollie.'

'I buried it — yes — I said a prayer — buried it — ' The voice died away. Mollie was struggling for breath now.

'She's going,' said Susan Grey,

moving forward. I turned away, stunned at what I had just heard, and unable to collect my thoughts. I was a foundling with no identity — an unwanted child, given away to Old Mollie, with a few gold coins! I felt Howard Tregarth's hand on my arm.

'Don't upset yourself too much, Miss Mountjoy.' I was trembling uncontrollably. Mollie did not speak again. Her life ebbed away very quickly, and, it seemed, peacefully.

'Here's the doctor,' said Abel Wilks. Dr. Fosset's bustling, cheerful presence was very welcome in that room.

'She's had a long life, and gone very quickly,' he said, in a matter-of-fact way. 'No burden to anyone.'

'I'll see to her, Doctor,' said Susan Grey. 'What about the funeral?' she asked me. I was so dazed with Mollie's revelations that I felt quite unable to cope with such matters. Mr. Tregarth seemed to realize this, and I heard them making arrangements concerning Mollie. Barnaby began to howl, which brought me quickly back to the present. 'What's going to become of him?' I asked.

'He'll come and live at Abinger Hall, of course,' said Mr. Tregarth.

'But . . . you don't like dogs. Not around the house, anyway.'

'There are several dogs living there, as you know. He will be well cared for in the stables.'

'And tomorrow,' I said, 'it's the harvest supper. What will happen now?'

'The harvest supper will go on as planned. It will not be the funeral until two days afterwards. Mrs. Grey has agreed to look after things.'

Some time later, still feeling stunned, I sat in the dogcart with Howard Tregarth and Barnaby, who was whining miserably. I thought of how I had grown up in the mill-house, believing myself to be Clare Mountjoy, and I had been living a lie. But if I was not Clare Mountjoy, who was I?

Although I tried very hard to control my tears, I found it quite impossible, and wept quietly for most of the journey back.

'Please, Miss Mountjoy, don't distress yourself so. I know it's been an awful shock for you. It's natural you should want to find out your true identity, if the story is true, and strange though it is, it may well be true. I've heard the most incredible true stories in court. If there is any way at all in which I can assist you in finding out more, I will do. She could have attended the young woman's confinement in any of the large houses in the district, and there are quite a number, as you know. I don't know much about the villagers, but I know she was considered quite a queer old character. If the remains of the other baby could be produced, naturally, the whole affair would take on a different aspect. I must confess I see no reason why she should take an oath like that, and then tell a lot of lies. She certainly had nothing to gain by that confession, only a clear conscience. I will accompany you to the funeral, don't upset yourself too much. She was very old, you know, and quite active up to the end.'

Mr. Tregarth gave me such comfort as he could on the way back, but it was easy for him, I thought. He knew beyond all doubt that he was Howard Tregarth; his whole position in life hinged on that simple fact.

I had believed myself to be the miller's daughter; I had loved my mother and grandmother, but now I was not sure that they had been related to me at all. But who was I? We arrived back at Abinger Hall, and Barnaby was left with the stable-boy. I heard him barking disconsolately as we walked away.

'Now you have a busy day ahead tomorrow,' said the Squire. 'Try and get some sleep tonight. It will all seem so much better in the morning.'

Glancing upwards, I saw the new moon in the old moon's arms. Mollie had always said that was a sure sign of bad weather to come. I went to my room. I reflected that I'd had some tormenting nights since I'd lived at Abinger Hall, but this must surely be the worst of them all.

12

The next day dawned fair and sunny, and I rose after a restless night, with my thoughts still in a turmoil. On top of Mollie's revelations, I had the worry of wondering how Miss Hepton would take it when Mr. Tregarth told her I would be acting as hostess for the harvest supper. For in spite of the shock I had received the previous day, I knew that he still wanted me to. What would people think, though, when they knew Miss Hepton was back at Abinger Hall? They would expect her to be hostess.

My worry concerning her was speedily resolved, however. During the morning I heard that she had a severe headache, and would remain in her room for the rest of the day. She was, apparently, not at home to anyone. It was a relief to me. I wondered what Mr. Tregarth had said to her. Whatever it was, it had certainly been effective. I still felt dazed by Mollie's disclosures, and subsequent death, but I tried to lose myself in the present. I had told Dorothy, very briefly, that Mollie had died, but that she was very old, and had not been ill for more than a day or so. The child looked somewhat surprised, but she did not comment. Anyway, there was far too much excitement going on with the harvest supper for her to pay much heed to such things, which was just as well. She did, however, look pleased when I told her that Barnaby had come to live at Abinger Hall.

Trestle tables had been put out at the back of the house, for the villagers. They began to come through the gates shortly after noon, all smiling, and in their Sunday clothes.

George Hansbury was there, with his wife and daughter, Polly. Abel Wilks arrived in his waggon, and to my surprise, I saw Polly flush, and seem overcome by shyness at the sight of him. He had brought Susan Grey with him and they told me that they had carried out all Mr. Tregarth's instructions concerning poor Mollie's affairs. I thanked them both.

'You'll thank me with a dance, later on, I hope,' said Abel Wilks. I said that I would think about it, and he lounged off, smiling, to talk to some of the village girls.

'Is everything proceeding satisfactorily?' asked Mr. Tregarth, who was busy engaging different people in conversation. His voice was tender as he spoke to me.

'Everything seems to be going very well, sir. The women with young children are pleased that they are not missing anything. They can enjoy themselves this afternoon, and go home later.'

Certainly everyone seemed to be enjoying themselves. After the old Squire being such a recluse, all Bramwell was delighted to take part in the harvest celebrations. The fact that the present Squire was going among them, and taking an interest in them personally was such a novelty that they found it hard to believe. Moreover, his daughter was running and playing with the village children, and he didn't appear to mind at all. Barnaby came lolloping round from the stables, and lay on the grass, watching proceedings. The men drank their cider, and there was much good-natured talk and chaffing on all sides. I felt a pang of guilt about Miss Hepton, but I knew that this would not be her idea of enjoyment at all.

As for myself, although I smiled and mingled with the villagers, all the preparations I had made seemed to have been made in another lifetime. My whole world had been turned upside down by a few words spoken by a dying woman.

Throughout the long, hot afternoon, cider and beer was drunk, and endless urns of tea were made in the kitchen. Although the domestic staff at the Hall were working hard, they were joining in the merrymaking, too. In the evening I changed my cotton dress for the new, cream taffeta one, and Dorothy wore her pink one. Guests began to arrive for the ball, which was to be very informal. Mr. Tregarth thought it better to dispense with cards for booking dances.

The Boldwoods arrived, with Roger looking out for me eagerly, also several other families who lived in the neighbourhood. Outside, the fidlers and flautists from the village began to tune up.

The trestle tables were loaded up again for the villagers, and inside the house a cold supper was laid out in the dining room. The hall looked charming, decorated with flowers, foliage, coloured paper and corn dollies. The musicians began to play, and Mr. Tregarth came straight up to me, and asked me to dance with him. I was whirled away in his arms, and in no time at all the floor seemed to fill up with laughing, dancing people.

'You look very nice, Miss Mountjoy,'

said Mr. Tregarth. 'I am grateful to you for the way you have carried things off for the harvest home. I know what a strain you are under. Ah, I see Dorothy is dancing, too.'

Yes, she was being taken round by a smiling village boy. I had given her some dancing lessons, and she seemed to have a natural sense of rhythm. I saw Abel Wilks dancing with Polly Hansbury, and saw the look of happiness on her face. It occurred to me that the quiet, shy, Polly might be the very girl for him.

'Is Miss Hepton not even able to come down for an hour or so?' I asked Mr. Tregarth, somewhat timidly. I felt a bit sorry for her.

'There is nothing wrong with Miss Hepton. If she chooses to sulk in her room, then that is her affair,' he said. 'Miss Boldwood was asking if she could see her. I said that we had merely been told that she was not at home to anyone. I am not going to run Abinger Hall to suit her.'

I could quite see his point of view. Certainly, we were managing very well without her. As we danced, the clasp of his hand on mine, and the closeness of our bodies filled me with an almost unbearable joy. On top of the shock of Mollie's death, and the knowledge that I was not Clare Mountjoy, I felt that things were reaching a crisis between Howard Tregarth, Miss Hepton, and myself. When the music stopped, he gave me a little bow, after he had escorted me to my seat, and said he would be back before long.

Abel Wilks and Roger Boldwood both came hurrying towards me at the same time. Roger Boldwood reached me first.

'My dance, I hope, Miss Mountjoy.'

'Mine next time,' said Abel Wilks, not in the least abashed. He grinned at me as I moved onto the floor with Roger Boldwood. Someone else was dancing with Dorothy now, whirling her around, while she squealed with laughter.

'Miss Mountjoy,' said Roger, 'I have

something which I would like to say to you in private. I am sure we could manage a few words away from everyone.'

'Is it important?' I asked.

'Well, yes, or I would not mention it.'

'Perhaps later on we could speak together, then,' I said. I could not help noticing that he was holding my hand more tightly than was necessary, and that his eyes were just as admiring as Mr. Tregarth's.

'You look lovely, Miss Mountjoy,' he said. 'You are an ideal hostess for the harvest supper.' Little did he know the state of inward turmoil that I was in.

'It's taken a lot of organizing,' I said. 'I knew that the mothers with young children would not be able to come tonight, so we made sure they would enjoy themselves this afternoon.'

'You have been very elusive lately, Miss Mountjoy. I've been to the house on several occasions, but I haven't seen you.'

'That is scarcely surprising. I am, after all, Dorothy's governess.'

'You seem to fit in with the life at Abinger Hall,' he remarked, after a pause. 'I suppose you must have some free time.'

I smiled. 'I do have some, although Dorothy is very reluctant to allow me to.'

The floor was getting more and more crowded. The waltz came to an end. 'I shall see you later, Miss Mountjoy,' said Roger Boldwood, giving my hand a squeeze.

'Now it's my turn!' cried Abel Wilks triumphantly, a few minutes later. He danced extremely well, I noticed. With his slightly swaggering manner, and swarthy good looks, I could well imagine him having a devastating effect on the village girls. He had been drinking; enough to make him a little merry.

'I've only come here to be with you,' he said.

'I find that rather hard to believe.'

'You had a trying time last night. I suppose I heard things that I shouldn't. But you can trust me not to gossip about it.'

'Thank you,' I said. 'I don't think Mrs. Grey will gossip, either. But in any case, as what Mollie said concerned me, Mr. Tregarth wanted independent witnesses there.'

'Yes, I can understand that. But you must feel — '

'Please!' I said. 'I am very upset about Mollie's death, apart from anything else. Let me get the harvest supper over — and her funeral. I am very grateful to you for being so helpful. I am very glad that you moved into the mill-house when you did. You seem to be a very self sufficient man — well able to manage alone.'

'I can manage alone — for some things.' This remark was accompanied by a saucy smile. I could see Mr. Tregarth eyeing me with my partner as we danced past him. He was dancing with Polly Hansbury now. She was dressed in her best muslin gown, her face a little solemn at finding herself in the Squire's arms. Abel Wilks refused to release me for the next dance, and I wondered if this idea of not having engagement cards was a good one after all.

'You can't keep dancing with me all the time,' I said reprovingly.

'Given the chance, I could. I'm getting black looks from certain quarters, I know.' I guessed he meant Roger Boldwood. While I was thinking this the music stopped, and there was a short interval in the dancing, while the musicians had some refreshments. Abel Wilks thanked me for the dance, and asked if there was anything he could get me.

'Thank you, no. Our refreshments are in the dining room,' I said.

'I understand. You are not one of the villagers.' He said this quite banteringly, yet it disturbed me a great deal more than it would have done, before I had heard Mollie's story. I could tell by

Abel Wilks' face that he realised his teasing remark had not been very tactful. He withdrew without attempting to make amends, which was really the best thing to do under the circumstances.

Dorothy came running up to me. I tied the bow of her sash again, as it was half undone, and she said she was hungry. We went into the dining room together, where there were groups of people standing and sitting, partaking of the refreshments. I had allowed Dorothy to help me arrange the flowers on the dining table, and the masses of blooms made a beautiful display. The butler and footman were on duty there, but the atmosphere was very informal. There was every imaginable savoury and sweet to choose from.

'Now then, Miss Dorothy,' said Simkins, 'what do you want?' He loaded up a plate for her. I selected a few dainties for myself, while Mrs. Boldwood chattered away somewhat disjointedly.

'Isn't it all splendid? And so informal. Kate is enjoying herself — but what a shame Celia is ill! And Dorothy is enjoying herself, too. These patties are delicious . . . where is Roger? Oh, here he is.'

Her son walked into the room, and I guessed he had seen me leave the hall. 'So — it's refreshment time,' he said. 'I suppose you are eating my share, Dorothy.' She gave a muffled giggle, but could not speak because her mouth was too full. Mrs. Appleyard appeared then, saying that she was looking for her husband.

'I expect he's outside. It's quite lively out there,' remarked Roger, helping himself to a drink. It was lively everywhere; the sound of music and dancing filtered through to the dining room. Roger insisted on getting me a glass of wine. I sipped it slowly. Dorothy was boasting about the fact that she was getting asked to dance a lot, and that she had danced with her father.

'You may dance as much as you like, Dorothy, but your father says you are not to go outside,' I told her.

'You can go outside, though, can't you?' asked Roger Boldwood, in a low voice. 'I must see you alone.'

What did he want? Was it just an excuse, or had he really something to tell me in private? He brought me another glass of wine, although I had not requested it, and only drank it out of politeness. It seemed to be going to my head, just a little. But why not? It was the harvest supper, and most people were having a drink to celebrate. Then I began to feel somewhat strange. It seemed stiflingly hot in the dining room.

'I think I would probably feel better for a breath of fresh air,' I said. Mrs. Boldwood obligingly handed me her fan. I wafted myself with it, but I still felt strange.

'Have a walk outside,' suggested her son. 'I'll escort you.'

'Mind you don't catch a chill,' was

his mother's advice to me. 'Have you a shawl?'

'Yes.' Somewhat gropingly I picked it up.

'It's so easy to get a chill in the night air,' said Mrs. Boldwood.

Closely followed by Roger Boldwood, I went outside. As he had remarked, it was certainly lively out there. There were lanterns to light up the scene, which was one of carefree merry-making. People were eating, drinking, and dancing about, while one man from the village played his fiddle as if he were there for the night. The sound of laughter and snatches of song came from all directions. I took a deep breath of the cool night air, and suddenly my knees were weak.

'I don't feel very well,' I murmured. 'I feel — '

'Walk a little. You will feel better soon,' said Mr. Boldwood, coaxingly. He put his arm round my waist, and began to lead me away from the house. I did not feel any better, though. My head felt so strange, and I no longer seemed in full possession of my normal senses. I allowed him to lead me along, away from the scene of feasting and merriment. Then, with a sudden, unexpected movement, he pulled me behind a clump of trees, and began to shower kisses on my face and neck.

'Miss Mountjoy — you are lovely — adorable! If you knew how much I admire you — want you! Kiss me! Kiss me!' He held me in a tight grip, with one hand under my shawl, caressing my bare shoulders and neck. His mouth was pressed hard on mine; the urgency of his desire was plain. I felt as if I were going to faint, there and then. He pushed me down into the dew-wet grass.

'Mr. Boldwood, please! Stop!' I gasped. 'I'm not well — take me back to the house!'

'Nonsense! Why do you think I've brought you away from the house?'

I was really frightened by now. 'Let me go! Let me go!' He put his hand over my mouth.

'Stop making noises, do. You must have known what to expect when I asked you to come out.' He kissed me again, even more passionately.

'Please! Let me go,' I begged, trying to push him away.

'Stop playing the great lady with me. I know your background — you're only one of the villagers — ' As he spoke, he was suddenly hauled off me with furious strength.

'What are you doing out here with Miss Mountjoy?' came Howard Tregarth's voice, with so much anger in it that it was like a whiplash.

'Oh — er — Howard — she felt a little faint, and I brought her out for a breath of fresh air — ' Roger Boldwood broke off lamely. With Mr. Tregarth's help, I struggled to my feet. He stood in the dim light, his attitude so enraged and so menacing, that I felt I had not known him until this moment.

'How dare you?' he said to Roger Boldwood. 'Your behaviour is beneath contempt. You are a guest in my house, otherwise . . . ' I thought that he was going to knock the other man down, but he appeared to control his anger with a tremendous effort. 'Come, Miss Mountjoy,' he said.

He took my arm, and I walked along unsteadily. Roger Boldwood slunk away silently.

'Have you been drinking?' asked Mr. Tregarth, the anger still in his voice.

'Only two glasses of wine, which Mr. Boldwood gave me, but they made me feel ill — I don't feel well at all — '

'He must have made up a fine mixture for you! I've no doubt he knows some pretty tricks — but he's not going to use them in my house. You are going to bed now. I'll get one of the maids to take you and Dorothy to your rooms. No, better still, I'll take you both myself.'

Back in the house, he sat me in a chair, and speedily appeared with his protesting daughter. He took us both up to the nursery. I sank down into the big, shabby armchair, feeling sick, ill, and exhausted. He told me he would get a maid, and after some time, during which I could not be bothered to reply to Dorothy's prattle, he came back with Rosie. She seemed a bit flushed and giggly, but she soon got Dorothy to bed.

'Miss Mountjoy is not very well. Will you assist her to bed?' he asked, when the maid reappeared from the night nursery.

'Very well, sir.' This she did, leaving me alone in bed, with the darkness swirling all around me. I lay there, feeling ill and dizzy, and utterly weary, with the shock of Mollie's death now coming to the forefront of my mind, and the things she had said before she had died. On top of that, I'd had to put on a bright front for the harvest supper. And then, Roger Boldwood's behaviour, and Mr. Tregarth's anger . . . I lay there in a sick daze, with everything going round and round in my head.

It was still dark when I was roused from slumber by a loud peal of thunder. I sat up in bed, startled. Then I heard rain beating on the window, and I knew that the long spell of dry weather had ended in a thunderstorm. I lay down again, but roused periodically at the sound of the storm, until the rolls of thunder died away. It was very late before I woke the following morning. There was a knock at my bedroom door, and Rosie appeared with a breakfast tray for me. Dorothy was with her.

'Good day, miss. Are you better today?' was Rosie's greeting.

'Are you better, Miss Mountjoy?' asked Dorothy, and I was suddenly moved to see anxiety in the sharp, dark eyes. For Dorothy knew, even at her age, that a person you loved could become ill, and not get better just because you loved them.

'I am much better today,' I said. 'I shall have my breakfast in bed, and then I shall get up, and we will have some lessons as usual.'

'The master said you were not to be disturbed before eleven o'clock,' said Rosie. 'It's raining very hard. Miss Dorothy has been eager to see you.'

'I expect she has,' I said. 'As for the rain, well, the harvest supper is over, and all is safely gathered in.'

'Yes, miss,' said Rosie, with a twinkle in her eye. 'They do say there was some gathering in to do last night, after the harvest supper.' She left the room, and Dorothy perched herself on the bed.

I wondered if Rosie had been making an oblique reference to the way Mr. Tregarth had brought Dorothy and me up to the nursery, and asked her to help me to bed. Still, it was no use wondering what the servants thought about things at Abinger Hall. It was more to the point to wonder what the Squire thought about finding me with Roger Boldwood last night. Mr. Boldwood had tried to take advantage of me because he thought he could get away with it. I guessed that Mr. Tregarth had missed me, gone searching for me, and been enraged at what he had found. I sipped a cup of tea, and thought again of the anger in his voice. I had a dull, throbbing headache, and felt terribly depressed at the thought of Mollie's funeral on the morrow.

We spent what was left of the morning quietly, but after luncheon a message came for me to see Mr. Tregarth in the library. No doubt he wished to speak to me in connection with Mollie's funeral. I wondered if he would blame me at all for Mr. Boldwood's behaviour. With some misgivings I tapped on the library door, and entered the room.

'Be seated, Miss Mountjoy. Isn't it a dreadful day? I'm afraid there will be some flooding if it doesn't improve. How are you today?'

'Much better, thank you, sir.' I felt rather embarrassed. 'I'm sorry about last night. Perhaps I should not have gone outside — '

'It was not your fault,' he said, almost brusquely. 'I am very glad I went looking for you. Put the matter to one side, Miss Mountjoy. I have been to Bramwell this morning.'

'In this awful weather?'

'Certainly. It was necessary. You acted as hostess last night, in spite of the business of having to rush to Mollie's cottage the night before. It was only right that I should attend to certain matters in connection with the funeral. It is at two o'clock tomorrow. I shall drive there with you, and afterwards we had better go back to the cottage. I expect there will be a few things to be sorted out there.'

'Thank you, sir. There is only one thing — ' I hesitated.

'Yes?'

'Do you mind if Barnaby comes with us?'

'No. You can bring the dog, if he is any comfort to you.'

We discussed Mollie's funeral for a bit longer, and then he went on to say how everyone had enjoyed the harvest supper. He did not refer to the incident with Roger Boldwood, and I did not bring it up again. Afterwards I went back to the schoolroom, thinking that there was still no sign of Miss Hepton around the house.

After hours and hours of drenching rain, the wind suddenly rose, and tore with fury across the sodden land. Summer seemed to have passed in a night.

13

It was raining on the wind when Mr. Tregarth and I drove into Bramwell the following day, for Mollie's funeral. Barnaby sat quietly in the carriage with us. The ditches on either side of the lanes were runing with water; the sodden hayricks had been hastily covered with canvas, and the cattle stood in the fields, miserable looking, squelching in mud.

'I hear one or two trees have been blown down,' remarked Mr. Tregarth. 'The rain and wind between them have done a fair amount of damage. Pyke says we'll get more rain — he can tell by his rheumatism.'

He spoke cheerfully, in an attempt to cheer me up. He knew this was not a happy occasion for me by any means. I was grateful to him for accompanying me to the funeral, though. As we drove along, I remembered my grandmother's funeral, and her last words: 'Unconsecrated ground — like a dog'. The mystery of my birth tormented me as I sat there with Howard Tregarth. That, and my unspoken love for him, and my hunger to know if he cared for me too . . .

So we made our way, in the wind and rain, to the church at Bramwell. I was pleased to see Abel Wilks there, and Susan Grey. A few of the other villagers were there too, to pay their last respects to the strange, witch-like old woman, who had lived in that cottage as long as anyone could remember. Barnaby sat silently outside the church, during the service. Afterwards, we left the churchyard, and Mr. Tregarth, Susan Grey, Abel Wilks and I went along the muddy river bank to the cottage. Mrs. Grey said she would make us a cup of tea there.

'Oh, look!' I exclaimed. 'The willow tree has been uprooted by the wind.' It had crashed down into the river.

It seemed symbolic, somehow, now that Mollie was no longer there.

We entered the cottage. How desolate everywhere looked. The poor old woman had said she wanted me to have everything. As if she had anything of value to leave! Mrs. Grey had lit the fire, and she now proceeded to boil some water in Mollie's kettle. Barnaby had entered the house with us, but was now scratching at the door to be let out again. I opened it, and he ran outside.

'Have you brought the key to the trunk with you?' asked Mr. Tregarth. When I said I had, he remarked that it might be as well to open it as soon as possible. Accordingly, when we had drunk our tea, the two of us went upstairs, and into Mollie's bedroom. He pulled the trunk out from under the bed, and I unlocked it. How well I remembered that trunk, and how Mollie had produced some lace and material from it to help me out with my wardrobe when I had first gone to Abinger Hall. Mingled with the musty smell from it was the faint perfume of lavender, and I guessed that my grandmother had kept her supplied with it.

Most of the stuff inside the trunk was useless. Old clothes, even old shoes, several pieces of china, and right at the bottom, a worn leather bag. I opened it, watched by Mr. Tregarth. There were a few gold coins inside.

'There's some money inside,' I said. 'And — yes — a bracelet!' For a long time I stared at it, after I had pulled it out of the bag. I looked at Howard Tregarth without speaking, and he looked at me.

'You recognize it?' he said at last.

'Yes,' I whispered. 'Do you?'

'Yes. Put it back in the bag.' I gave a long, last look at the unusual, rather oriental looking bracelet. It was in the shape of a snake, with dull red stones for eyes. It was made of some very tarnished metal, probably silver. I felt suddenly nauseated, remembering the remains in the Blue Room, and the human bone which I had seen, with an identical bracelet hanging on it.

'I think you have the main item of interest to you now, Miss Mountjoy,' said Mr. Tregarth quietly. 'You can decide what you want to do with the rest of the stuff later.'

Dazed with the shock of what I had found, I followed him downstairs. I heard myself thanking Susan Grey and Abel Wilks for being so helpful. I felt all I wanted to do just then was to get back to Abinger Hall. There was a scratching at the door, and I opened it, to let in Barnaby. He was growling, and had something in his mouth.

'What have you got? Drop it,' I said. He dropped a bone at my foot, and bounded outside again.

'I should think that dog wonders where he do live now,' remarked Susan Grey, putting on her shawl. 'He'll have to settle down at the Hall now.'

'Yes. He settled down with Mollie quite well,' I said. We all prepared to leave the cottage. Barnaby reappeared, growling again, with another bone.

'Where is he getting them from?' I asked, in exasperation.

Mr. Tregarth stepped outside, into the windswept garden. The tears filled my eyes, as we left the cottage. I was trembling with shock. I locked the door behind me.

'Wilks! Come here!' Mr. Tregarth's voice was so urgent, and the look on his face so strange as he shouted from down by the river, that Abel Wilks hurried forward immediately. I followed him, and so did Susan Grey, to where the Squire was standing, beside the uprooted willow tree. Barnaby stood there barking. In the mud were bits of rotted wood, a pile of tiny bones, and a little skull.

★ ★ ★

'Be seated, Miss Mountjoy,' said Mr. Tregarth. 'Er — have you brought the bracelet?'

'I'm wearing it,' I said simply, and

held out my wrist. Carefully cleaned, the bracelet gleamed silver now, and the red stones seemed to wink in the firelight. There were two tiny catches on it which linked it to the twin bracelet which I had seen on the skeleton in the Blue Room.

It was the day after Mollie's funeral, and Mr. Tregarth had asked me to see him in the library that afternoon. I had slept little throughout the night, and although he did not comment, it seemed to me that his glance took in the pallor of my face, and the weariness about my eyes.

'Knowing you, Miss Mountjoy,' he said with a smile, 'I've no doubt you intend to take Mollie's story — and your half of the bracelet — to a higher authority, to try and get the whole mystery cleared up.'

'I have thought of doing that, sir,' I admitted. 'It's only natural. After all, I saw the same bracelet in the Blue Room, with my own eyes.'

'Precisely. But I think I can clear up

the mystery for you.'

He produced the diary, marriage certificate and letter which I had found in the sealed up book. He handed me the letter, and once again I read the anguished words, written so long ago: 'I ask you to help me now, for pity's sake . . . what is to become of us? You cannot be so cruel . . . '

'Your mother,' he said. 'Francoise D'arcy, before she married Anthony Tregarth.' He handed me the miniatures. 'Your parents.'

I sat without speaking, completely dazed, and yet wanting to know all sorts of things. But Mr. Tregarth had evidently been sorting out a number of facts in connection with my parentage. He opened the diary at July the twenty-third, eighteen sixty-two. ' "The evidence was removed',' he said, quoting from it. 'You were the evidence, Miss Mountjoy; you were handed over to Mollie. That was the night of your birth.'

'No, it was July the twenty-second — ' I began, finding my voice.

'No, the Mountjoy baby was born that day. Within twenty-four hours she had died, and you took her place. Naturally, you were told it was the twenty-second.'

'Then — I've no name at all!' I exclaimed, in sudden realization. 'I was never baptised! I was handed, nameless, to Old Mollie.'

'I'm afraid so. But you are the daughter of Anthony Tregarth, and the grand-daughter of Lionel Tregarth. Just for interest, it seems that we are distant cousins — third cousins, I believe.'

'It could have been any of the big houses in the neighbourhood,' I said in a low voice. 'But it was this house — this house! Then she — my mother — was actually living here. And — ' I broke off, and tried to collect my thoughts. The mystery of my birth had been solved quickly, unexpectedly, and rather frighteningly. 'That girl was my mother,' I said. 'She died when I was born! Why was she walled up like that?

It was as if she had never been — '

'Precisely,' said Howard Tregarth, drily.

It was all too much for me. I burst into tears. Then, to my amazement, Mr. Tregarth rose, and came to me. He put his arm round me, and held me close. 'It's an awful shock for you, I know. Dear Miss Mountjoy — Clare — '

His voice stopped, but in spite of the shock of finding out my true parentage, I felt my whole body trembling at the sudden contact with his. He began to speak again.

'On the twenty-third of July, besides saying the evidence was removed, it says in the diary that the cause of the trouble left also. I believe that was a reference to your mother's death. Then there is no entry for three days, then one which says everything has been attended to. 'What is done is done now. Only I know the truth. May God forgive me.' Your mother had died as secretly as she had lived here, and her body had been concealed in the wall. As you remarked, it was as if she had never been.'

'But why not a coffin, at least?' I asked, tearfully.

'For obvious reasons. You can't order a coffin without the undertaker wanting to know certain details.'

'But how could your uncle have kept a girl here secretly?'

'My uncle — your grandfather, don't forget! I guessed there was someone here who had an inkling that strange things happened that night. I had a feeling that the coachman was none other than our friend, old Pyke himself — fifty-five years service, man and boy. I had a very long talk with him this morning.' My sobs had ceased now, but Mr. Tregarth still remained with his arm round me. He went on speaking, his voice gentle: 'Pyke kept repeating that he would have done anything for the old Squire, but after a while, when he realized that no harm could come to him, he told me that Uncle Lionel used to have a valet, Moffat, who was devoted to him, and who died about three years ago. He told me that there was quite a lot of gossip in the servants' hall at one time, and some of the servants said there was someone living in the Blue Room, as it was called. Apparently in those days they had a cook-housekeeper called Mrs. Brown, and she and Moffat seemed to be in some sort of conspiracy. The valet took trays of food upstairs every day, which he said were for the master. There were whispers that certain garments appeared in the laundry, which could not have been worn by the master. There was, too, talk by some of the maids that the sound of sobbing had been heard coming from the Blue Room.'

'Probably that's how the talk of it being haunted started in the first place,' I said musingly.

'No doubt. Anyway, Pyke said the valet came to him one evening, and asked him if he knew of a midwife. He said he knew of Old Mollie in Bramwell. Moffat said that they must drive there, but that they were both pledged to secrecy, and must be masked, and that the midwife must be blindfolded. They brought Old Mollie, blindfold, into the house secretly, and took her to where this girl was lying, in the Blue Room. There was no sign of my uncle anywhere. Pyke had been told to go back to the stables and wait. He waited a long time, until at last Moffat appeared. He told Pyke he would receive five sovereigns if he kept quiet always about what he had seen and heard that night. Pyke agreed, and together they returned to the Blue Room. The young woman was obviously dead, still and silent on the bed. The baby was alive, and Pyke waited while Moffat bribed Old Mollie to take the child and be gone. Finally she agreed to do so, and they blindfolded her and drove her back. They wore masks all the time. Moffat knew that Pyke could be trusted, and he explained to him in confidence that the young woman had been the Squire's son's wife, but that the Squire wanted the whole thing keeping quiet. Apparently the girl had been left destitute, on account of her husband being cut off without any money, and the fact that he gambled any money he had, anyway. After his death she had thrown herself on the mercy of her father-in-law, and he had secretly and grudgingly sent her some money. He said this was only until after the child was born, but she had used the money to come to England, and to avoid the embarrassment of her making herself a nuisance, he had secretly taken her into the house, on the understanding that once the child was born, she was to take a sum of money and leave the country for good. Undoubtedly she hoped his heart would melt towards her, and that once the child was born, they would make their home here, and the grandchild would eventually inherit Abinger Hall. But his son's behaviour had broken Uncle Lionel's heart. He could not forgive that girl — a little French dancing girl of no family or good connections — for marrying his only child. Despite his grief for his son, presumably, after her death, his only thought was to get rid of the child of that union.'

'And Pyke has known all this, and remained silent all these years?'

'He has. What would he have gained by gossiping? He presumed that the girl had been buried, secretly and decently.'

'So she could have been,' I said.

'Yes, she could. But her name would have been in the church records, even though her grave had been unmarked, and neglected. My uncle wanted no trace of her existence left.'

* * *

'And yet, he kept her marriage certificate.'

'I've no doubt the poor girl showed him it, to prove that they were really married, and that the expected child was his legal heir. I suppose he knew that she would never be discovered during his lifetime, and that it would not matter afterwards. Something made him keep these few things, even though they were well hidden away. But this is not all I wanted to talk to you about.'

'No?' I asked wonderingly. I thought that it all seemed a dream, listening to this strange, sad story, and feeling Mr. Tregarth's arm around me.

'Miss Mountjoy, I must tell you I have had certain feelings towards you for a long time — right from the start, I think. I wanted to wait until after the harvest, to make sure that what I felt for you was no passing fancy. Clare, I love you, and I want you for my wife!'

I could see that he was deeply moved; that what he was saying was not being easy. For a moment I could not take it in, although I had dreamed of it; longed for it. I could not believe that I, the miller's daughter, was being proposed to by the Squire. Straight away the thought came that I was not the miller's daughter though, after all.

'Mr. Tregarth . . . I can't believe you really mean it.' To my dismay, I began to cry again. He didn't seem to mind, though. He was in a very emotional state himself. The next moment we were in each other's arms, and there seemed to be no need for words.

'My darling,' he murmured, after what seemed a long time. 'My first marriage was not happy. I was very wary, so I waited, and watched you, and loved you, and my feelings grew and grew . . .'

'So did mine,' I admitted, in a muffled voice. 'But I don't see how you can marry me — your daughter's governess — ' then I broke off, still trying to take in the fact that I was not the miller's daughter, but a Tregarth, the same as he was! He drew me close to him, kissing me again.

'I have the right to choose my own wife. My first wife was considered eminently suitable, and brought me nothing but heartache. If people gossip at first about our marriage, does it

334

matter?' As he spoke, there was a flash of lightning in the room. 'Another storm coming up,' he said. 'We've certainly had some bad weather since the harvest.'

The next minute a peal of thunder crashed out, loud and ominous, accompanied by the now familiar sound of rain.

'I've left Dorothy in the schoolroom. She may be frightened,' I said.

He smiled. 'And that's another thing. You love Dorothy, and she loves you.'

'But what about Miss Hepton?'

'What about her? She cannot go on living here permanently. I shall have to make the situation known to her, although I don't wish to make a public announcement just yet. We will tell Dorothy together, when things are more settled. I know all this is a lot for you to cope with all at once. The truth about your parentage, and the fact that I love you, and want to marry you. Are you happy, my darling?'

Was I happy? I was so many things at

once. The tears were still wet on my cheeks, and yet I felt joy as I left the library and went up to the schoolroom. The overwhelming thought was that Howard Tregarth truly loved me, just as I loved him, but I still felt rather dazed at knowing that it was to Abinger Hall that Mollie had come, late one night, all those years ago. I was actually a distant cousin of his! But now I knew that he had cared for me right from the start, and that his feelings had grown . . .

'How long will this rain last?' asked Dorothy, dolefully.

'I don't know, I'm afraid. We've had a good summer, Dorothy. It couldn't go on for ever.'

'We won't be able to go out.'

'I'm afraid we won't,' I agreed. Just then I did not care about such trivial things. I had discovered my true parentage, and Howard Tregarth had proposed to me.

'Come on, let's get on with the history lesson,' I said, a little absently.

It rained all day. It was still raining

when I took Dorothy down for dinner. Once again, Miss Hepton was absent from the dinner table.

'Is Miss Hepton still unwell?' I enquired.

'She appeared briefly about half an hour ago. Since then, however, she seems to have suffered a relapse,' said Mr. Tregarth, with rather a wry smile. I guessed then that he had told her certain things. Would she pack up immediately, and leave Abinger Hall? Strange; she had always regarded me as a rival, even in the days when I had thought it ridiculous. How she must hate me now! She had grown up here, and had staked everything on winning Howard Tregarth's love, and remaining here as mistress. Even the servants knew it; surely he must have known it too. And yet, I felt instinctively that he had never allowed things to get out of hand between them. Out of politeness, he had waited for her to make the decision to leave, and as she had made no move to go, it must have put him in a decidedly unpleasant position. Had he asked her to leave? I wondered about this during dinner. When the meal was over, Mr. Tregarth asked me to join him and Dorothy in the library, and the three of us went there together. We played games with Dorothy, and my heart was bursting with happiness. I thought it had been the most wonderful day of my life.

True, my origins were sad; it would take me a long time to get used to the idea that I was a foundling. But still, I knew now *who* I was, even though my poor mother had wept and been unhappy, shut in the Blue Room during the long months before I was born. Still, she had loved me, I told myself, and put one half of her bracelet on my tiny arm, before she had died. When Howard looked at me now, there was no mistaking the affection in his eyes, but although there was a new understanding between us, Dorothy did not seem to be an intruder. Rather, we all seemed even more of a family together.

After she was in bed, at Howard's request, I returned to the library, and we spent the evening together. There were so many things I wanted to tell him about, and so many things I wanted to ask him. I sat on his knee in the big leather armchair, and he talked to me of his first wife, and of his life in Italy. What he told me tallied closely with the information Dorothy had given me. He said they lived there because of his wife's health.

'She imagined I did not know about this man she used to visit,' he said. 'I knew, but I did nothing about it, because although she had not made me happy, I pitied her, and I knew she had only a short time to live. When the end was near, I brought that man to see her, much to his surprise. For a long time I had felt no love for her, only pity, so there was no jealousy.'

I realized then that I need never fear rivalry from his dead wife.

'Today seemed like a dream,' I said. 'So much has happened. I know who I am now, although it will take me a long time to get used to the idea. There are still some things I don't know — '

'There is much we don't know — much we will never know. But Mollie's story seems to stand.'

'It is so sad,' I said, after a pause. 'And although I never mentioned it at the time, I did hear sobbing when I had the Blue Room, before the remains were discovered.'

'Oh, come now, darling! It must have been the wind, or something.'

'I knew you wouldn't believe me. But I did — and I was very glad to move out of there.'

He kissed me. 'If you insist there was sobbing, I will have to believe you. In view of all the other strange things which have happened in this house, I should not discount your story.'

His voice was tender, but I knew that he was discounting my story. I was so happy, though, that it did not seem to matter. I did not stay late in the library, as Howard thought that I had had a very trying few days, which was true. I was very tired. But as I ascended the staircase that night, it flashed through my mind that before long I would ascend it as mistress of Abinger Hall. And all this had come about because I had received a letter telling me to quit the mill-house, and I had gone to the Squire myself, to put my point of view before him.

14

For the following few days the weather did not improve at all. It confined us all more or less to the house, and Miss Hepton appeared to be keeping to her room constantly. The findings in Mollie's garden were now in official hands; a pathologist stated that the remains were those of a very young baby.

'When the police have finished,' I said to Howard, 'I would like the vicar to say a few words over the remains, and for them to be put in the church-yard. Mainly for my grandmother's sake.' Then I remembered she was not my grandmother, but, still I had loved her as such. I told him of her strange, sad, last words: 'Unconsecrated ground . . . like a dog.'

That broken, whispered sentence had puzzled me for a long time, but I understood it very well now.

'Certainly we will have that done,' he said. 'There are quite a number of things to be settled, I'm afraid. The weather is still abominable, and I still have the problem of Miss Hepton on my hands. I don't know what her plans are, but as soon as the weather improves, I shall ask her. She cannot stay here indefinitely.'

The wind had dropped, and it was raining again. Dorothy was becoming very difficult just now. She could sense that I was preoccupied, as was her father, and, moreover, it was days since she had ridden out on her pony, or gone for a long walk. She was naturally active and restless, and we'd had one or two scenes in the schoolroom, during one of which she had flung her books on the floor. Unfortunately for Dorothy, her father had come into the schoolroom unexpectedly, and witnessed this. He said she would not be permitted to dine downstairs again until he thought fit. I thought this a bit harsh, and Dorothy set up a loud wail of protest. However, I could not go against her father's wishes, and that evening she was left to dine alone. I went down to dinner feeling rather upset about things. To my surprise Miss Hepton appeared in the dining room, immaculately dressed in a grey gown, but looking a trifle wan and pinched in the face. She exchanged greetings with me, but the cold hatred in her eyes when her gaze met mine was unnerving. She had tried to win Howard Tregarth for her husband; tried and failed. And I had succeeded; I, the miller's daughter. But no, I was not the miller's daughter . . .

'I trust you are feeling better,' said Howard politely, addressing her.

'Better?' She gave an unpleasant laugh, and sat down.

'I am afraid we are having a spell of exceedingly bad weather,' he went on 'Social life has been drastically curtailed.'

'I should imagine you are not very interested in social life just now,' she said sourly. I saw Howard's face change, as he realized that Miss Hepton was in a vile temper. She was merely making a pretence of eating. If she had to leave the house to her victor, she was not going to leave quietly, and in a well bred manner, from what I could see. She shot me another baleful glance.

'I hear that old witch of yours has died,' was her next remark. 'With a baby's skeleton and all buried in the garden. Well, well, doubtless she was useful to you — '

'Will you please leave this table?' Howard was obviously trying to control his anger. 'You have not just come out of your rooms to insult Miss Mountjoy with servants' tales — '

'Servants' tales?' She blazed hatred at me. 'What is she, if not a glorified servant? You'll be the laughing stock of the county, if you marry her.'

'No, Miss Hepton,' said Howard, his voice dangerously quiet. 'If you behave in this manner, *you'll* be the laughing stock.'

'Stock — you talk of stock! There is some rotten stock in the Tregarth family! Smuggling went on in this house at one time — I know! Your uncle told me about Rogue Tregarth — '

'That's going back a few generations,' he interrupted her. 'I can't be responsible for my ancestors.'

'It's as well you can't. I've heard some pretty stories whispered about this family. As for your uncle, my, he had a guilty conscience in the end — '

'For heavens sake, go back to your rooms! Please keep to them until such time as you leave the house for good.' The only other time I had seen my future husband so angry was when he had hauled Roger Boldwood off me. He stood up, glaring at Miss Hepton. She rose, too, and turned her venom on me.

'As for you, you little fool! Do you imagine for one moment that Howard Tregarth loves you? He's ensuring Abinger Hall remains in his hands! Oh, yes, he explained to me how you had discovered your true identity, and I

346

know as well as he does that his uncle left no will. That means the whole estate goes to the next-of-kin — and he isn't going to give you the chance to take your case to the High Court! He loves Abinger Hall, not you, and to keep it, he's prepared to ruin his life — and mine.'

'Yours?' I stared at her.

'Yes. We were happy enough until you walked in, with your insipid sweetness, and he knows it. We were destined for each other — but make no mistake, you were reared a miller's daughter, and a miller's daughter you will always be. Your mother was a cheap little dancing girl — do you really believe that is a fitting basis for a lady of the manor?'

'Will you please go?' repeated Howard.

'Go?' Miss Hepton moved away a couple of paces. 'Yes, I don't wish to sit at the same table as that woman.' Then she delivered her parting shot at me. Her pretence of insulting the Tregarth family fizzled out, and her true feelings were exposed. 'Why don't *you* go, and leave us both alone? Together we can repair the havoc you brought to this house with your snooping and prying, and spying. Marry Abel Wilks, the miller. You'd be a fitting wife for him, I've no doubt.'

With that, she walked out of the room. I sat, feeling stunned and sick. I looked across the table at Howard, and somehow things were different between us. I had been wildly happy at the thought of becoming his wife; I had never dreamed that his proposal could possibly have been prompted by any reason other than the same love for me which I felt for him. But seeds of doubt had been sown. He had some knowledge of the law; I had none.

'Don't upset yourself on her account,' he said, but I could see that he was upset and still angry himself. But was his anger because Miss Hepton had told a few home truths? 'I had no idea she could be so vindictive,' he went on. 'She was helpful and charming at one time.'

'She was helpful and charming until I came on the scene,' I said, in a low voice. 'She's been jealous of me right from the start. I always knew she wanted you to marry her.'

'It occurred to me that she had certain ideas in that direction shortly after I took over Abinger Hall. On one or two occasions I've had to make a firm stand — in fact, I've been close to snubbing her. I used to think that after the harvest I would make it plain that she could not expect to live here indefinitely. She is not penniless, and she could make her home with her aunt any time.'

'I suppose she will, now.'

'Wherever she goes, she will not be staying here much longer. Meanwhile, ignore her outburst. I'm glad none of the servants were present to hear her. We can talk about our future plans, perhaps.'

I would have been overjoyed to do so, just a short while before, but Miss Hepton's outburst had upset me too much to do anything like that. The mere thought of food was nauseating. I pushed away my plate, and said I had a headache, and if Howard would excuse me, I would like to go to my room.

'Yes, of course, Clare.' He stood up. 'You've had a trying time lately, and this has been an upsetting day.'

I tried to smile, and bidding him goodnight, I left the room without a kiss between us. I felt that I wanted to be alone to think about what Celia Hepton had said. I was no longer sure that Howard Tregarth loved me for myself. He had assured me that he had intended to propose to me after the harvest, in any case. Those tender glances which he had cast in my direction for many weeks now — had they really indicated that he wanted to marry me? Or, as I had sometimes suspected, was he merely hoping for an enjoyable flirtation with his daughter's governess?

Could I believe that if I had not come to Abinger Hall, he would really have asked Miss Hepton to leave, after the harvest? Or, as she had intimated, would they by this time have been officially engaged?

How quickly he had interviewed Pyke, and winkled the whole story out of him after we had realized that bracelet Mollie had left me was identical to the one found on the remains. He had gone to a lot of trouble, and produced everything, cut and dried, for me. I had thought he had done that for my sake, but having pieced the story together for me, he had lost no time in proposing. By making me his wife, he would foil any attempt on my part to establish sole claim to Abinger Hall.

My brief, ecstatic happiness melted away as if it had never been.

★ ★ ★

The following morning there was a letter for me, readdressed on from the mill-house. I looked at the postmark as

I took it up to the schoolroom, and saw that it was from Plymouth. I sat reading it, while Dorothy struggled with her writing, and the rain came steadily down. It was from Mrs. Thomas, my former employer, telling me that the governess they had replaced me with had left, and they wondered if there was any chance at all that my circumstances would permit me to go back now.

It seemed to me as I read it, that this letter was an omen. It was offering me a way out. I had spent two happy years with the Thomas family, while the months I had spent at Abinger Hall had been chaotic, despairing, ecstatic, and wretched in turn. I thought how unhappy my poor mother must have been in this house. The old story of the Tregarths being an unlucky family came back to me. Quite suddenly, I saw the course which I should take.

I would tell Howard Tregarth that I thought we had been too hasty in deciding to get married. I would let him see that he need not presume that because he was the Squire, any woman he cast his eyes on would be eager to become his wife. I did not want him as a husband, if he did not care for me without any ulterior motive. Miss Hepton had opened my eyes with her outburst. I would leave Abinger Hall — leave it, with all its unhappy memories, and make a new life for myself in Plymouth.

But Dorothy . . . I looked across at the dark head bent over her books, and felt a lump in my throat. It would be a wrench to leave her. As for her father, well, I would have to starve my love for him, until it died away. While I was sitting thinking this, Rosie came with word that Mr. Tregarth wished to see me in the library. Instantly, despite my plans, I found myself yearning for his love and tenderness. I rose, and went downstairs, outwardly composed, despite my thudding heart. I knocked formally on the door, and he bade me enter, speaking briskly, in the old way. I had planned to be cool when I spoke to him, but I now found that *his* manner had changed completely from that of the solicitous husband-to-be.

'Good day. I trust your headache is better, this morning?'

'Much better, thank you.' It was not strictly true, and I could not help thinking that he looked rather drawn in the face himself. 'I wished to see you,' I added quickly. 'I've been thinking things over, and I've decided that perhaps we should not rush into things too hastily.'

Was it my imagination, or did he go a shade paler when I said that? But his voice when he replied was bland and controlled.

'I quite understand,' he said. 'Indeed, I am of the same mind myself. I should of course, have let you know your legal position before, but it is not too late. As my uncle did not leave a will, you understand that the next-of-kin can claim the estate. As far as I can see, you are the grandchild, the next-of-kin.'

The warmth and tenderness had

gone completely from his voice.

'My grandfather never wanted me,' I exclaimed, almost to myself, feeling, even after twenty years, the pain of rejection.

'These things do not count at all,' was the cool rejoinder. 'The law deals with facts, not emotions.'

Realizing how his manner had changed towards me, a hot pride and anger began to rise in me. He was bound to say something after Miss Hepton's outburst of the night before, and it seemed to me he was saving face by discussing my claim to Abinger Hall now. His voice expressionless, he said that the identity of Francoise Tregarth could be established, and that there were witnesses who could give evidence on my behalf. 'If you decide to pursue your claim,' he went on, 'it could be quite costly. But you may well find a solicitor willing to defer his fees until a settlement has been made — '

'Thank you,' I said, interrupting him. 'I must get back to the schoolroom now.' I stood up, my cheeks burning, and hurried from the room, before I displayed emotion in front of him. He had obviously assumed that I would be interested in claiming Abinger Hall, after what Miss Hepton had said. He had told me the bare facts, and warned me that it would be costly to pursue my claim. He and Miss Hepton both wanted Abinger Hall — well, let them have it, then. I would go back to the Thomas family, and try to forget. Try to forget the findings in the Blue Room. Try to forget Old Mollie's story. Try to forget Dorothy. And most of all, I would try to forget that golden summer, before the harvest, when I had longed for Howard Tregarth's love, and he had touched my hand, and everything had seemed magical and unreal . . .

The following morning I looked out on leaden skies again, although the rain had ceased. I had not been downstairs to dine the previous night, but had stayed with Dorothy in the nursery. I told her we would go riding that morning. 'Just up and down the drive,' I said, 'as everywhere is so damp.' I knew that her father was in Chollerford that day, sitting on the Bench. She brightened up a bit as we exercised our mounts, but she was still not herself. She was upset, I knew, because of her father's displeasure with her. I told her we would not be going out again that day, but after luncheon, she asked if she could go for a walk. 'Alone,' she added, knowing that I had no intention of trudging through the sodden parkland. We had ridden up and down the drive until I was tired, and it was extremely wet underfoot everywhere. I welcomed the chance to be alone by the nursery fire for a short time, and to consider Mrs. Thomas' letter, and think about replying to it. At the same time, I didn't really want Dorothy to trail around the damp, cheerless parkland by herself.

'Can't you play with Violet?' I asked. 'It's not really suitable for walks today.'

'I can take Barnaby with me, though.'

'Very well. Just walk up the drive, and around the stableyard with him, though. Don't be long.' I helped her on with her outdoor clothes, and off she went. I resolved that we would have toasted crumpets in front of the nursery fire for tea. For some time I sat with Mrs. Thomas' letter on my knee, thinking about things. I felt that some of the servants must have guessed how tense the situation was becoming at Abinger Hall.

Tired after two sleepless nights, I must have dozed off beside the warm fire, and woke with a start, to find that Dorothy had been absent for more than an hour. I had not thought she would be gone for more than half that time, and decided I had better go downstairs, and see where she was. I put on my outdoor clothes, and went downstairs. At the stables they said they had seen her, and she had gone off with Barnaby, but that had been some time before.

'Will you have a look round for her, please? I only thought she would have been gone for a short while.' Old Pyke sent the stable-boy off to look for her, but I was beginning to feel anxious. I would try the servants' hall, just in case she had gone there to be made a fuss of. I knew she sometimes did this. But in the servants' hall they had not seen her.

Within the next hour the gardeners, footman, stable-boy and all the manservants were searching the grounds for her. Dorothy had disappeared, and so had Barnaby. I felt sick with apprehension. What would Howard Tregarth say if he returned from Chollerford to find his daughter missing? Just for once I had not accompanied her on a walk, and this was the result. While I was in the hall, wondering if any of the men had found her, Miss Hepton came in, wearing outdoor clothes. She approached me straight away.

'What's this about Dorothy being missing?' she enquired. I was surprised, yet glad in a way that she had spoken. Perhaps she was sorry about her behaviour of the previous night.

'She went out to take my dog for a walk,' I said. 'I expected her back long before this. It's very worrying — I'm hoping she will be found before long.'

'I've been out, and I can tell you she's not in the grounds.'

'I've told them to look up by the quarry,' I said.

'I'll make sure she's not hiding in my apartments,' went on Miss Hepton. 'I'll warrant the little minx is hiding. She hid in the house once before, when she hadn't been here long. I managed to find her that time.'

We both agreed to search the house for Dorothy, and meet in the hall again if we couldn't find her. Our search proved fruitless.

'There is only one place left,' said Miss Hepton. 'If you like, we will go there together. There is a big cellar under the house, and more than one way of getting to it. There is a way from my apartments, the most convenient way, actually. We shall have to take a candle.'

'If that is the only place left, by all means,' I said. 'Although I'm sure she would not dare go down there. Really it would be better if one of the men searched there.'

'They are still searching the grounds.' I followed her to her apartments, where she lit a candle, and took me along a corridor.

'I know every inch of this place,' she explained. 'As a child I explored it again and again. Dorothy is a bit like that, too, curious. I know all about the different ways to get down to the cellar, and I wouldn't be surprised if she does.' Quite suddenly she stopped, and stooping down, rolled back a piece of carpet. To my surprise there was a trap door underneath, which she unfastened and lifted up with apparent ease. She held up the candle, and I saw steps going down.

'I'll hold the candle. If you can go down, just a few steps, and shout for her, if she's there she should answer.'

Gingerly I put down my feet, and

slowly began to descend, looking round all the time. There was an overwhelming smell of damp and mustiness; of dust and decay. It was most unpleasant. I descended a few steps.

'Dorothy!' I called, straining to see in the darkness. 'Dorothy!'

'Here, take the candle a minute,' suggested Miss Hepton. She handed it to me. 'Dorothy!' I called again, holding it aloft. The next moment the flame was almost extinguished with a gust of air, as, with a merciless clop, the trapdoor came downwards, and imprisoned me in that eerie place.

'Miss Hepton!' I shouted. 'Miss Hepton, let me out! Open the door! Open it!' Holding the candle in one hand, I banged on the trapdoor with the other. Then I put the candle on a step lower down, and shouted and pushed at the door with all my strength. There was no reply. Panic rose in me. What a fool I had been to trust that woman! I should have known that she had not put her hatred of me to one side merely because Dorothy was missing. I was locked in the cellar now. Locked in, and who was to know where I was? Nobody, but Miss Hepton. For a long time I stood on the steps with my head near the trapdoor, shouting and banging. Then it occurred to me that she had no intention of opening that door again. I had better try to find out if there were any other means of escape.

Trembling with fear, I gingerly descended the steps, and, holding the candle aloft, I gazed round at the place I was in. This was not the cellar, though, I soon realized that. I was in a passage several feet high, and six or seven feet wide. There was no light anywhere save that of the candle, and the air was damp, foul, and musty.

'Dorothy!' I called, and heard my voice echo weirdly. She was certainly not down here. If I walked along the passage, though, I might find somewhere else to come out of. Fearfully I began to walk along, thinking in terror that when the candle went out, I would be left in total darkness. I would die in this dreadful tomb! I walked along for what seemed an age. Every so often I stopped and listened, in the faint hope that Miss Hepton would relent, and open the trapdoor, and call for me. But no such thing happened. The tunnel was bound to lead somewhere, though. And then, in the ghostly light of the candle, the tunnel terminated in a door. It appeared to be made of iron, though, stout and impregnable. I banged against it, and shouted, but to no avail. When I had satisfied myself that it was of no use to try and get out at that end, I reasoned that the only thing to do was to retrace my footsteps, and see if things were any better at the other end. It was wet underfoot as I walked along. I was thankful that I had a good, slow burning candle with me.

I told myself not to panic. It was just an unpleasant trick on Miss Hepton's part. There must be another way out somewhere; of course there must. I walked on and on, past the steps which

I had come down, and along in the opposite direction. The tunnel seemed interminable; wherever did it lead to? The dank, foul smell seemed to grow stronger and stronger. At last I reached what appeared to be the end of it. I could feel water seeping through my boots. There was no way out, though. I stood and shouted, and heard the futile echo of my own voice. What was I going to do? What would Howard Tregarth think when he came home and found both Dorothy and me missing? Would he ever find me? Would that woman tell him where I was? And where was Dorothy? Automatically I made my way back to the steps. How long would the candle last, and how would I endure being alone down here in the dark? There must be rats here, I thought, with a shudder. Did the Squire even know this tunnel existed?

I sat on the icy cold, stone steps, and tried to collect my thoughts. I banged the trapdoor again and shouted, but there was no reply. There must be something I could do, but I knew that there was not. Either I was rescued, or I stayed there and died. The tunnel was not straight, I noticed. It seemed to curve at a certain point. Where did it come from, and where did it go to? Suddenly, I realized where it came from. Dorothy had told me there was a door in the disused quarry, and I had told her she was not to go down there. She said it was covered up with stones.

So this tunnel ran from the quarry, and under the house. But where did it go to then? I sat, trying to think rationally about this, but all the time I knew that it didn't matter were it went. I was still trapped down there, in that airless, foul smelling atmosphere. After a while I stood up, and thought I would try walking along the tunnel again, but not in the quarry direction. I began my miserable journey a second time. I had no watch with me, so I had no idea of the time, although I seemed to have been there an eternity.

I walked on and on, listening to the

hollow echo of my footsteps. Suddenly, ahead of me, I saw a peephole of daylight! I began to run, overwhelmed with joy. Miss Hepton had evidently realized that her horrible joke had gone far enough. It was fortunate that I had walked in that direction. The daylight was blotted out now, but there was a hissing, gurgling noise. I held the candle up high, and tried to see ahead. I gave a scream of terror at what I saw. Water was pouring into the tunnel, flooding it! A blind horror filled me, such as I had never known. I ran back to the steps as fast as I could. Perspiration was trickling down my back, and my heart was beating as if it would burst. I knew now where the tunnel led to. It led from the quarry to the river, where Dorothy had noticed that door, and it was possible to open it, and let the water in. I could hear my breath coming in sobs as I ran along. At one point I nearly stumbled; the candle flickered wildly, but some-how I regained my balance. At last I found the steps, and hurried up them. How long would it take the water to penetrate to where I was? How deep would it be? The silly, schoolroom phrase came back to me, about water finding its own level. How far up the steps would it creep?

I sat, in frozen fear, waiting for the first, inexorable trickle to appear. It did so, and I sat there motionless, watching it rush unchecked through the tunnel. I knew that this had not happened by chance. Miss Hepton would know all about this tunnel, and how it could be flooded. I guessed that she had gone out of the house as soon as she had replaced the trapdoor, and hurried across the sodden grounds to the river bank. She knew a great deal more than Howard Tregarth about Abinger Hall; she boasted that she knew every inch of it. Fate had played into her hands, with Dorothy being missing. My throat felt parched as I crouched there. In desperation I shouted again and again, and banged on the trapdoor. The water was swirling round the bottom step now. Would it flood through, and fill the entire tunnel? In terror I pictured myself drowning in that dreadful place. Left there, I would either drown, or starve to death. I knew the river was swollen by the heavy rains. My only hope of survival lay in the chance that there would be no rain during the next twenty-four hours, and the level of the water would drop. Perhaps then I could wade through it to the opening, and see if there was any means of escape from that point.

But how high would the water rise, before it began to recede? I crouched there, trembling, as the candle burned lower and lower. If only I had my watch on me . . . had they found Dorothy? Had Howard Tregarth come back from Chollerford yet? My head swam with disjointed thoughts. On and on came the water; it was up two steps now, and still coming in. How could Celia Hepton do anything so wicked? I changed my position on the steps. Rats and all sorts of things must be coming in with the water! Any woman who could do such a thing as leave anyone trapped in a place like this must have murder in her heart.

I was beginning to feel very tired, in spite of the fear which kept me alert. I must not be tired, I told myself. Above all, I must not faint. I must keep high up on those stone steps. As the hours went slowly by, I grew more and more weary, and yet I knew that my only hope of getting out of there alive was to keep calm, and hope the water would not get too high. It still came in, covering up step after step. It was up to the third step already. It was like a nightmare, and yet I knew that it was real. Tears of panic and fear and loneliness rolled down my cheeks. I prayed with all my heart that something, somehow, would lead to my discovery. No wonder the Tregarths were not considered a very lucky family. As the water rose higher and higher, I screamed in terror, but there was nobody to hear my cries. I remembered Mollie's prophesy that the river took three lives every year, and another life was due to it. Mollie . . . the little bag she had left me, containing all her worldly wealth, a few gold coins, and what was far more important, the other half of my mother's bracelet. I counted the steps that were left uncovered, and there were seven. Her strange story came back to me vividly, yet as if it had all been a dream. She too had counted the first lot of steps the men had taken her up, and there had been ten. Ten steps. There were ten steps up to the trapdoor . . . but they could not have brought her here. Yet she said they had brought her along a place where their footsteps had echoed, but to bring her from the other end of the tunnel, they would have had to go down the quarry, and she would certainly have remembered that. A steep slope, rough ground . . . what a muddle it all was. But what did it matter now, anyway? Somehow she had been brought secretly to Abinger Hall, and I had been born. I had been born a Tregarth.

Fate had sent me to this house, and I had learnt the secret of my birth. I had experienced sudden happiness, and then heartbreak and disillusionment. Must I now pay the ultimate penalty for being the true heiress to Abinger Hall? My jumbled, feverish thoughts ran on and on. Who could I really trust, now that my ancestry was known? Could I really trust Howard Tregarth? Were he and Miss Hepton plotting my destruction between them, skilfully and unobtrusively?

The water seemed to have stopped rising now. In the last, guttering light of the candle, I could see this silent blackness all around me. Soon the candle would go out, and I would be left here in the dark. How long would I be able to huddle on this step, without food or water, and without sleep? A short while later I was in entire darkness, and I sat there, desperate, despairing, but somehow clinging on. I forced myself to look straight ahead, and to keep very still. I told myself that the level of the water would drop; it was bound to drop. How long I remained there, praying and hoping I had no idea, but suddenly there was a noise overhead. Immediately I began shouting for help. I heard a dog bark, and the sound of the trapdoor being opened.

Howard Tregarth's face, white with fear, looked down at me.

'Oh, God, Clare — ' he broke off, and reaching down, helped me out of that terrible place. I remember being lifted out, and then everything went black. When I came round I was lying on a sofa in the drawing room, with Howard bending over me, and Barnaby slobberingly licking my face. The sharp tang of smelling salts was under my nose.

'She's coming round, sir.' That was Rosie's voice. How white and haggard Howard's face was . . .

'Clare,' he said softly. 'You're all right now. You're safe now.'

I could hear myself sobbing. I was gulping down some fiery liquid.

'Bring her a light meal and a hot drink, Rosie,' I heard him say. And then I felt his arms around me, and his lips on mine. I knew then that I was safe again, and my terrible ordeal was over.

'My darling! My darling! It's been dreadful!' As my senses gradually cleared, I knew that this was no pretence of love on his part. We clung together, kissing and murmuring words of endearment. The coldness and misunderstanding between us melted away as if it had never been.

'But what about Dorothy?' I asked, remembering other things.

'She's safe, too. Abel Wilks and George Hansbury's daughter brought her here in his waggon last night. He really is a most excellent man, and she's a sweet girl. Dorothy had some scheme of running away with Barnaby. She wasn't seen going through the lodge gates, because she and the dog climbed over the wall. She said you were going to go away and leave us; apparently she'd read a letter which you had left in the schoolroom, asking you to take up your former position. The fact that she is getting on so well with her reading proved a mixed blessing under the circumstances, I'm afraid. She wanted to go to Chollerford, but Barnaby turned back, and went to Bramwell. She was too obstinate to come home — you know what these Tregarths are like — so she went trudging on with the dog, and, quite naturally, ended up at the mill-house. Here comes Rosie with some food and a hot drink for you.'

'Last night?' I exclaimed, glancing at the clock. 'Why, it's morning!'

'Yes. The house and grounds had been searched — I've been up all night — ' He broke off. 'Eat your breakfast.' Rosie left the room, and I drank the coffee, and ate the egg, kidney and bacon which she had brought. My eyes were pricking with weariness, and I was shivering.

'How did you find me, then?' I asked.

'In the end, that silly old dog found you. I gave him one of your slippers, and he promptly chased all round the house with it! But it was a last resort, my darling. I kept encouraging him to find you, and we followed him all over the place. In the end, though, he went along the corridor that leads off from Celia's apartments, and stood barking. I pulled up the carpet, and there was the trapdoor. I didn't even know about it — oh, Clare, if we had not found you — '

'I would have starved, or drowned, thanks to Miss Hepton.'

'Drowned? Miss Hepton — Celia?'

'Yes. She led me there. She said Dorothy might know of that trapdoor. She said it was another way of getting down to the cellar. All the men servants were searching the grounds, so she held the candle while I went down a couple of steps. I shouted for Dorothy, then she handed me the candle, so I could look about me, and closed the trapdoor. I soon realized it was a tunnel, and not the cellar at all. I knew where it ran to at one end — I guessed it was the disused quarry, because Dorothy had told me there was a door there, hidden by stones. Then I turned and walked in the other direction — ' I recounted to him my dreadful experiences, and how I had guessed Miss Hepton had opened the other door, and let the river flood in.

'And where is Miss Hepton now?' I asked.

He hesitated before replying. 'She was missing too, when I came back from Chollerford. Her maid didn't know where she was. It's been the most appalling business, dearest. Pyke said he had seen her going towards the river bank, and thought she was looking for Dorothy, like everyone else. No fewer than three people missing — can you imagine what a state the place was in? Then Dorothy was returned safe and sound — and then, early this morning — yes, our friend Wilks again — he saw a body caught on some reeds near the mill-house. There was a rowing boat drifting downstream, too. He notified the police, and drove here again. I had told him that you and Miss Hepton were missing when he brought Dorothy back, and he said he would keep his eyes open. He was able to tell me that the drowned woman was not you, thank heaven. Tessa, Celia's maid, went to identify her mistress. I certainly don't think she drowned intentionally — ' he broke off, and shook his head.

For a moment I was speechless with shock. 'How dreadful,' I said at last. 'I think she must have gone completely out of her mind in the end. She was obsessed with the idea of being mistress here.'

'Try not to brood about all this just now,' said Howard gently. 'You had better go to bed. All that matters to me is that you are safe. Rosie will look after Dorothy — and I will tell her not to mention Celia's death to the child.'

I willingly complied with his suggestion that I should go to bed, but many thoughts ran through my mind before I fell into an exhausted slumber. Not least was the realization that Abel Wilks had proved of sterling worth. It was to the gentle Polly that he had turned, to accompany Dorothy home. Somehow I felt, that despite his hitherto roving eye, it was Polly who would become his wife. They would both be in good hands, I reflected.

★ ★ ★

That evening, after a long sleep, but still feeling tired and stiff, I was re-united with Dorothy in the nursery. She was quiet and white-faced, and I resolved that I would not scold her for running away and causing so much trouble. I did, however, rebuke her for reading other people's letters. 'Because Mrs. Thomas has asked me to go back,' I explained, 'it doesn't mean I shall be going.'

'And you're not? You're going to stay here with Papa and me?'

'Yes. Always,' I said, giving her a little hug. She flushed with relief and joy. It was plain that she had suffered intensely at the thought of losing me, and by her father's displeasure at her for throwing her schoolroom books on the floor. However, she was allowed to come downstairs for dinner that evening. She sat pale and silent throughout the meal, and the three of us went to the library together, afterwards. Howard played a game with her, and I sat resting, watching them. We kissed her goodnight after half an hour, and Rosie put her to bed. As soon as we were alone, Howard sat in the armchair, and took me on his knee.

'Did you really intend to leave, and go to Plymouth?' he asked.

'I was considering it,' I admitted. 'After what Miss Hepton said, I wondered if you really did love me, or if it was just Abinger Hall you wanted.'

'And you were going to go away, and nurse your pride?'

'I suppose I would have done.'

'I spoke to you like that in the library, because I too wondered if it was only Abinger Hall you wanted, not me. I've already told you, I've been very wary of falling in love again, and I didn't want to have to entertain the least doubt about you. I thought I would soon know if you wanted me, or if you preferred to pursue your claim of being next-of-kin. But you behaved like a true Tregarth.' He smiled.

'Yes, and so did you. Proud; obstinate.'

'What happened to you, my darling, was a dreadful experience. But one thing it did was to make us both realize just how precious the other one was.'

'I think I realized how precious you were to me before that experience — but all I wanted was for you to find me, and tell me I meant more to you than Abinger Hall.'

'And you are convinced now?'

'Quite convinced.' We sat with our cheeks pressed together for a long time. 'As I sat in that tunnel,' I said musingly,

'I counted the steps, and there were ten. Old Mollie said the first lot of steps she had been taken up were ten, because she counted them. And she said her footsteps echoed before she went up the steps, so it sounded as if they had taken her along the tunnel. But they couldn't have taken her down the steep banks of the quarry, and she couldn't have come in the river end, so how did she get in?'

'I've been doing a bit of investigating myself,' said Howard. 'Pyke says that fifteen years or so ago, the rainfall was exceptionally heavy, and the river flooded so badly that it broke down the bank, and changed its course. Apparently the tunnel used to lead from the quarry out to a place near the landing stage. In the days when they used to quarry the stone, they used to take the stones right under the house, through the tunnel, and then put them on to the barges which used the river in those days. That was before the railways, of course. So even though the quarry was actually in the Tregarth grounds, and not all that far from the house, it was made as unobtrusive as possible. Also, at one time, I believe a certain amount of smuggling went on. As you can imagine, it was quite easy to smuggle stuff from the river barges, and get it secretly into the house, via the tunnel. After the river changed its course, the door which led to the tunnel was below water level. They moved the landing stage and boathouse further up the bank, and of course, the tunnel remained sealed up at both ends. I've had so many practical things to deal with since I took over — such as dry rot in certain places — that I've had little time to concern myself with places at Abinger Hall which are now obsolete.'

'So when they brought Old Mollie to the house, the door was not under water,' I said slowly. 'I see now. That is another mystery cleared up. The only mystery left is the sound of sobbing which I used to hear in the Blue Room.'

'I think I know the answer to that,

darling, now I know the state of Celia's mind towards you. Not only do her apartments have access to that tunnel, they also have stairs which lead up to the attics. That would be the way they brought old Mollie up to the Blue Room; no doubt your mother, too, was taken up that private way. Now when you are close to the fireplace in these rooms, you can hear a conversation going on in the room above, by people near the fireplace there. I know this because I once heard some workmen talking in the room above where I was sitting. I heard them quite distinctly. I think Celia used to go into the attic above the Blue Room, and sob into the fireplace. Or she may have got her maid to do it; they were as thick as thieves. When you moved into the other room, she could not get to the attic above so easily; in any case, by that time, she realized you could not be frightened away like that. There will, of course, be an inquest. It is all most unpleasant, and you had better get a good night's rest now, as you still have to catch up with a good deal of sleep.'

He was right about this, and there were lines of strain and fatigue on his face, too. They did not decrease over the next few days, either, as there was much to attend to. The verdict at Miss Hepton's inquest was death by misadventure. A hammer and chisel had been found in the rowing boat, which had just drifted on down the river. Miss Hepton had obviously taken the boat out with the intention of opening the door. It was assumed that she had overbalanced and fallen into the water; something which could happen quite easily, as she would be using all her strength to knock out the rusted staple. 'I've examined it, and that's what she did. Once the staple was broken, the metal rod bolting the door would come off, and the water would rush in,' explained Howard.

I shuddered. 'She would have had difficulty in keeping the boat steady,' he went on. 'Few women would have ventured out on a river to attempt what she did. The current must have caught her up and carried her downstream, before the first water began to rush into the tunnel.'

I didn't want to think about it. No one would ever know exactly what happened, and I felt it was better not known. 'She was spurred on by hatred,' I said. Pyke had attended the inquest, being the only person who had seen her going in the direction of the river. He said the river was over the bank in places, but he could see no reason for Miss Hepton altering the level of the water, unless she was fearful that the missing child had come to some harm there. Naturally, the fact that she had lured me down into the tunnel beforehand was something known only to Howard and myself, and we intended to keep it that way.

Informing Miss Hepton's ailing aunt of what had happened was not a happy task. In a way I was thankful that the poor lady was too ill to attend the funeral. Her niece had been laid to rest, and although there was still much to do in connection with her affairs, at least that was over. I had told Dorothy the bare facts, that Miss Hepton had unfortunately fallen in the river, and been drowned. I thought now that the atmosphere in the house should be made more cheerful for the child, and told her father so.

'Yes, we have all been through quite a lot since the harvest,' he said. 'And I think we have proved our love for each other.' He put his arms round me, and kissed me, very tenderly. 'I think we should go up and tell her that we are going to be married.'

We were in the library together, and Dorothy had been in bed for about half an hour. 'Shall we wait until morning?' I said. 'She may be asleep.'

'We'll go up to the night nursery, anyway.'

Arm in arm we walked slowly up the stairs together, and as we did so, I thought of Old Mollie, being led, blindfold, up those other stairs, long ago, to bring me into the world. I thought of my poor, lonely, unhappy mother. I reflected that her restless spirit should be at peace now; her child had come home at last, to be mistress of Abinger Hall. We entered the night nursery, to find Dorothy still awake, with Barnaby sleeping peacefully on the foot of the bed.

'Well, Dorothy,' I said, kissing her. 'We've come to tell you that your papa and I are going to be married very shortly, and you shall be bridesmaid! And I shall be your proper mother.'

'Is — is that really true, Papa?' she asked eagerly.

'It is indeed,' he assured her, smiling. 'But you mustn't read other people's letters again. It's wrong to do that.'

'I know, Papa. But I'm glad I did, because it made you want to marry Miss Mountjoy.'

Our eyes met over Dorothy's head. 'She's going to be a terrible handful for you,' her father said, but he was smiling.

'I knew that right from the start,' I said.

'I wished for this on my birthday!' cried Dorothy. 'You said if I didn't tell anyone, it would come true! I wished for you and Papa to get married, and it has come true! What did you wish for on your birthday, Miss Mountjoy?'

I could feel myself flushing.

'Yes, what did you wish for?' asked Howard.

'Oh, well,' I said. 'As you are both so curious, I wished for the same as Dorothy. So now you know.'

'And if it was your birthday, Papa,' pursued his daughter, 'what would you wish for?'

He slipped an arm round us both, and kissed us. 'I've nothing left to wish for now,' he said happily.

'And can Barnaby come in the house, and sleep here with me every night?'

'Yes, Dorothy. Barnaby has earned

the right to be part of the family.'
He smiled at me, and I knew that
the Tregarths would never be called
unlucky again.

THE END

We do hope that you have enjoyed reading this large print book.

Did you know that all of our titles are available for purchase?

We publish a wide range of high quality large print books including:
Romances, Mysteries, Classics
General Fiction
Non Fiction and Westerns

Special interest titles available in large print are:
The Little Oxford Dictionary
Music Book, Song Book
Hymn Book, Service Book

Also available from us courtesy of Oxford University Press:
Young Readers' Dictionary
(large print edition)
Young Readers' Thesaurus
(large print edition)

For further information or a free brochure, please contact us at:
Ulverscroft Large Print Books Ltd.,
The Green, Bradgate Road, Anstey,
Leicester, LE7 7FU, England.
Tel: (00 44) **0116 236 4325**
Fax: (00 44) **0116 234 0205**

WITHIN THESE WALLS

Susan Sarapuk

When Annie revisits Chattelcombe Priory, it's inevitable that unwelcome memories are stirred. It's where she'd fallen in love with Edward, and where Charlotte's accident, which changed everything, had happened. When Edward returns to buy the Priory, he also attempts to win back Annie. But Tim, the vicar, wants to turn the Priory into a retreat centre, and Annie finds herself torn between the two men. Then, she discovers a secret, which changes her perception of the past . . .

THE AUDACIOUS HIGHWAYMAN

Beth James

When Sophie once again meets her childhood hero Julian, who's been sent home in disgrace, she feels that romance has made her life complete. However, her brother Tom and his friend Harry must confine Sophie to her home because highwaymen have been sighted in the area. Sophie, contemptuous of the highwayman rumours, finds that any secret assignation with Julian seems doomed to failure. Then — when she's involved in a frightening encounter with the highwayman — her life is changed for ever.

DECEPTION

Fay Cunningham

When Alex bumps into Lucas Fairfax in Marbella all she wants is a story. So when she gets mistaken for his daughter's new nanny she jumps at the chance to see inside his sea-front villa. All's fair in love and journalism and a story about Lucas Fairfax, on holiday with his daughter, will be quite a scoop. But Alex didn't plan on falling in love, and now her deception is threatening to tear them apart.